Christmas in Bear Ridge

Sarah Wagner

www.BOROUGHSPUBLISHINGGROUP.com

CHRISTMAS IN BEAR RIDGE
Copyright © 2018 Sarah Wagner

ISBN 978-1-948029-54-4

*For my mother who had wanderlust but
too many commitments to be a nomad*

Christmas in Bear Ridge

Chapter One

Toni stared out the windshield of her nearly antique truck, watching the country go by, wishing she felt a connection to any of it. For her, this was the hardest time of year. Everyone was headed home to their families, no matter how many miles they had to travel. They saw nothing wrong with going halfway across the globe to spend a few days with people they worked hard to avoid during the rest of the year. It made no sense. And yet, a little part of her knew her real problem wasn't that she didn't understand, but that she *did*, and she was jealous of them all.

Most of the time, the little part of her that remembered what it was like to belong stayed quiet, allowing her to explore the world without any real responsibilities beyond the next beach, the next forest, the next mountain, the next town, the next job. Most of the time, her life was exactly what she'd always wanted. Until the day after Halloween when the world upchucked red, green, and silver everywhere, and every single radio channel spouted the same five weepy Christmas songs.

Tucking a loose strand of hair behind her ear, she stared into the darkening day, not headed anywhere specific. It didn't really matter where she went as long as it was away. Everything that mattered fit nicely in her truck-turned-tiny home, so it didn't really matter where she went. Work was easy to find if you weren't particular about the gig, and had a knack with people. Not that she needed to work, strictly speaking, but she liked to. As long as everyone knew it was only and always a temporary situation. She didn't do long-term anything—not jobs, not relationships, not even friendship. She knew better.

Time and experience gave some people roots. Loss had given her wings.

Melancholic nostalgia and sleepiness both reared their heads at once. She glanced in the rearview mirror and her eyes looked as bleary as they felt, with shadows beginning to creep across the skin beneath them. She figured she'd stop at the next gas station for a bit of a walk and some coffee before continuing on to Durango. Twilight came a little earlier in Colorado during December. It wasn't even four-thirty and the sky was darkening rapidly, and not only because of the heavy clouds moving in.

Ahead of her, nestled in the foothills of a smaller mountain she didn't recognize, a little town took shape as lights flickered on, sparkling against the snow in the fading light. It was definitely sitting right at the foothills, but she couldn't remember if it was the Rocky Mountains or the Grand Tetons, or if one was part of the other. Whatever else it was, wherever it was, the town was beautiful, and Toni was not so jaded as to be unable to appreciate that.

She turned off the main highway toward the town but couldn't outrun the storm. As she got closer to the lights, the snow started in earnest. At first, it was a little nerve wracking, but nothing she hadn't driven through before. The closer she got to the town, the heavier the snow. She thought about turning around, but pressed on instead, maneuvering through a storm that looked more like an old sci-fi movie's hyperspace effect than snow. She turned off her radio, like she needed to hear the road better, and slowed to a crawl as the snow began falling even heavier.

For a moment, she thought she was going to lose control of the Harvester, feeling the ice beneath the front tire as it spun then grabbed the snowpack before it did much more than shimmy. She gulped and patted the wheel tenderly. "It's okay, old girl. We can do this. It isn't much further and we should be in that town soon. It can't be too far."

Thankfully, the snowfall slowed until it was more pretty than treacherous. Big fat flakes drifted down from the red and orange sky in a beautiful dance. A large sign, lit by small, nearly hidden floodlights proclaimed that she was entering Bear Ridge. The sign looked quite old, carved into an enormous boulder on the side of the road. It said, "Welcome to Bear Ridge," in tall letters with a bas-relief of a mother bear and her cub in front of the mountain. In better weather, she might have hopped out and snapped a picture.

She drove slowly, still wary of the snow. At first, the houses were far apart, lone mailboxes marking their long driveways, little lights deep in the forest, bright yellow squares of warm light in the darkness occasionally accompanied by multicolored Christmas lights outlining the roofline. It was all quite sappy TV movie-esque. The road wound naturally through the woods, over a swollen creek, and then, suddenly, there was a quaint little town. Toni found herself humming "Over the River and Through the Woods," and smiled.

The town of Bear Ridge was adorable. It wasn't as thematic as Leavenworth or Aspen, or as muddled as a bigger town might be, but its age was definitely on display with its well kept but old Queen Anne Victorians and big brick mansions. Everything was decked out for Christmas. The tall black lampposts wore wreaths with great red bows, and every business seemed to have some bright display in its windows.

Out of the corner of her eye, she saw movement, a quick blur of grayish blue. She slammed on the brakes and swerved, trying to avoid the streak, or at least trying to slow down enough not to hurt it. The Harvester hit a spot of ice and spun into a tall yellow post in front of the gas station with a sickening sound, throwing her against the steering wheel as it came to a solid stop. For a moment, there wasn't much of anything, and then the pain bloomed in her head and face.

Her door flung open. "Are you okay?" a man asked.

"The dog. Did I hit the dog?" As if cued, a small blue pit bull started yapping and trying to climb up into the cab.

"Juni's fine. You missed her completely, and I'm grateful to you, but I really need to get a look at you."

"Oh my god, my truck." Tears welled in her eyes, joining the little bit of blood that was beginning to trickle down from the gash on her forehead.

"There's nothing about the truck that can't be fixed, I promise. I'm more worried about you right now."

Toni tried to focus on the man who was talking to her while his dog was trying desperately to climb into her lap, but finding focus was a little harder than it should have been. His blue eyes shined with concern and kindness. They were set in a handsome face with a strong jaw. He looked like every daydream of the perfect guy come to life. Everything drifted out of focus slightly and she felt a hand on her shoulder. For a moment she thought her dad was there, even though she knew that it couldn't be real.

"Nico," A voice called from somewhere else. "Everyone okay?"

"I'm not sure. You'd better call Doc Cait. She's bleeding." The man pressed some kind of cloth to her forehead, wiping her eyes. "What's your name, honey?"

"Toni. Toni Bell. Is the dog okay?"

"Yes. Juniper is perfectly fine. I should have had a better hold on her. In fact, I should have had her on a leash. She's never done that before. I'm sorry about your truck, but I'll do what I can to help you fix it." He leaned in a little closer, his breath warm on her neck. "My name is Nicodemous Panait. Everyone calls me Nico. We've called the doctor to come take a look at you, okay?"

Toni nodded slowly and leaned forward, laying her cheek on the steering wheel. She felt stupid being so upset about the truck. But it was hers, and her home. Yeah, but it could be fixed. "I think I'm okay, even if I'm bleeding. I think I—I need a minute."

"You're crying." There was panic in his voice.

Toni huffed out an annoyed laugh. "You're such a boy. I'm not crying because I'm hurt. This truck belonged to my parents. It's my home."

He looked at her strangely, stepped back and looked at the truck and back to her. "Your home? You can't be serious. It's a camper."

"It's more than enough for me." She sighed and unbuckled her seat belt. "I travel light."

"Stay put for a minute. Doc Cait will be here right away. I want to make sure you don't have a concussion or anything. Be still. The doctor is on the way. Where are you from, Toni?"

"Nowhere really."

"Everyone is from somewhere."

"I was born in Oregon, but I haven't had an address in almost five years. I have a friend who lets me use their mailing address for stupid shit like registration and taxes, but I don't live in any one place." She understood, at least peripherally, what he was doing, keeping her talking, making sure she was lucid. "I guess I'm a nomad."

"I come from nomads. I understand nomads. I didn't mean to be judgy or whatever, but it's hard for me to understand living in such a small space. My house is huge by comparison, and I'm plotting and planning all the time to put an addition on it."

"My family lived tiny before it was cool enough for a TV show." She laughed again and winced at the pain reverberating through her skull. "Well, half the time anyway." Her eyes felt a little heavy.

The man touched a lock of her hair. "This is a pretty color; is it natural?"

"What?" She couldn't believe he asked that.

"This coppery blonde, is it your natural hair color?"

He tapped on the door, loudly and she came to. She hadn't realized she'd fallen off.

"Huh? Um, yeah. I haven't done a dye job in a few years." She looked at him strangely.

"I'd really rather you didn't close your eyes right now and it looked like you were going to sleep. I panicked. Sorry if I scared you." He looked away for a moment then turned back to tell her, "Doc Cait is here. You're in the best hands there are. I promise."

The beautiful dark-haired man, did he say his name? Yeah. Nico. Right. Nico stepped aside and the man who replaced him was shorter and wilder, his graying curly hair shooting out in every direction. His green eyes were fearless and intelligent, and he had a smile that could make the Queen's Guard crack.

"What's your name, dear?" His voice was soft and soothing.

"Toni. Antoinette Bell." She flinched a bit when he shone a light in her face.

"Hello, Toni, I'm Doctor Cait. How old are you? Follow my finger with your eyes please." He held up a finger and moved it back and forth.

"Twenty-five." She followed his finger as he moved it. "How bad is it?"

"You've got a pretty nasty cut there and I'd really like to get it properly cleaned and treated. Can I take you to the clinic?"

"What about my truck?" Her fingers gripped the wheel tightly.

"Nico is going to get it towed to the best mechanic I know." His soft voice had a soothing tone, like it could rock her to sleep even as his thick fingers poked and prodded at her wound.

"I don't know him."

"I know, honey, but we need to get you taken care of and your truck isn't going anywhere without some help. I understand you don't know us, and that you have no reason to trust us, but I promise you, no one here is going to hurt you or take anything from you."

Even though Toni had heard all sorts of BS, she knew this guy was telling the truth. She nodded, and he gave her a small smile before he explained, "I'm going to reach across you and get your purse. Do you have a bag or something with clothes for the night?" He laid his hand on her head like he was taking her temperature the old-fashioned way, and for a brief moment, Toni swore his eyes changed color. Maybe she'd hit her head a little harder than she'd thought.

"This is my home." She heard the whine in her voice and got annoyed with herself. "I know you're trying to help. It's a little hard for me. I can get something together really quickly and I'll go with you. It's fine. I need to get into the back though."

"Are you dizzy?" He stared at her, narrowing his eyes while he held her face still. Again, his eyes changed. His pupils got huge, nearly eliminating all the mossy green before returning to normal.

"No, mostly I'm upset. I think I'm okay. Really. A little shook up more than anything."

"I understand, but I'd rather do it for you. I'll get in the passenger side and you can give me directions. I'm a doctor, I think I can manage getting your clothes together. I really need to get you over to the clinic."

"Really? I can't get my stuff by myself?"

"Not yet. Why don't you tell me what you need and where it is?"

Toni shut her eyes and felt the boom-boom-boom banging inside her head and capitulated. She told him where to find her backpack, the lockbox, which she wouldn't leave in the truck, her jeans, a sweater, a pair of sweats, clean underclothes, and her toiletry bag. She nearly forgot about her guitar, but he dutifully gathered her things together, and then handed the bag, the case, and her purse to Nico. "Nico will take your things over to the clinic."

"I can do it," she said and tried to get up.

"No, I really would rather you didn't. I've really got to get you taken care of properly." He took her hand and helped her stand. "I'm going to drive you over to the clinic and we'll get you stitched up, and I think we need a quick scan. Maybe I can close the wound up with glue. The scar won't be as bad that way."

"I don't care much about scars."

"A pretty girl like you? I don't think you'll want this scar." He opened the passenger door of a four-wheel-drive van. "I don't think you need to lay down on the gurney, do you?"

"No. I'm fine. I'm feeling so much better already." She pressed the cloth to her forehead, and when she drew it back and saw it was dripping blood, her stomach lurched a little. "Oh. Okay, fine."

"I take it you're a musician?"

"Sometimes. Not this time of year, if I can help it."

"Not a fan of Christmas?"

"The opposite really. I love Christmas." She didn't want to say any more. "You're a doctor?"

"I'm one of two here in Bear Ridge. I'm Dylan Cait." He smiled and looked at her almost expectantly, like she was supposed to understand something that she didn't. "Where were you headed?"

"Durango. I got an itch to head toward the Pacific and I've been making my way in that direction. I figured I'd reach Durango tonight and spend a few days puttering there before continuing on. I'd been on the road a while and needed a cup of coffee and a stretch. I saw the lights of the town and got off the highway."

"You saw the lights of this town?" His voice sounded incredulous.

"Yeah. That was before the snow hit, though. I wasn't expecting that. It all looked pretty clear when I turned off the highway. Then it was sort of like driving through a wall."

"I bet."

"It figures that I'd get through the snow without incident and crash to avoid a puppy." She sighed. "I always wanted a puppy."

"It's strange, actually," the doc commented. "Juniper is one of the best trained dogs in town. I've never seen her run from Nico before." He looked at Toni again, seeming to scan her. Weird.

"Am I missing something? Is there something going on that I don't know?" She looked at him, trying to tell if he was hiding something or if he was keeping her talking to make sure she was okay. "If I were really hurt, you'd have put me on the stretcher thing, right?"

"I don't think it's that bad, but it's my job to make sure, isn't it? I wouldn't be a good doctor if I wasn't certain you'd be fine before I let you leave my care." He shook his head as he pulled the van into the small parking lot in front of an older, box-style yellow brick building. He helped Toni out of the van and into the warmth of the clinic, and on into a small, clean, exam room. He gave her a more thorough exam, then he cleaned her gash up before settling on glue to hold her face together.

With instructions, a bottle of pain relievers, and a few dressing changes, Toni was done and sent out to the waiting room where Nico was waiting with her bags.

"I'm so glad you're okay. I'm so sorry. I really don't know what came over her. Juni has never done anything like that before." He smiled, looking a little sheepish. His long legs were covered in worn, stained jeans, and he wore a red plaid barn jacket dusted with melting snow. He extended his hand to her. "Nice to officially meet you."

"Juni's okay, though, right?" His hand felt good in hers—solid, warm, and lightly calloused.

"Yep. You missed her entirely. I promise. I had your truck towed over to Kevin's Garage. He's the best in town with older trucks."

"And mine is definitely that. She sighed heavily.

"I promise, if anyone can make it right, he can."

"Hopefully it won't put too big a bite in my savings." She couldn't imagine not getting it done.

"You wouldn't have had any repairs if it weren't for my crazy dog. Whatever it costs, I'll cover it."

Toni laughed. "Parts for an International Harvester are seriously hard to find. It's not going to be cheap."

"That truck means something to you, and it would be in perfect shape if not for Juni. I'll make it work, one way or another. I need to make this right."

"You know what? I'm not going to say no. But I am going to ask if you could give me a lift to a diner. I need to get something to eat and to find a place to stay for a few days while my house is under repair."

"Your house? You really live in that thing, like full time?"

"I don't need much, and I'm all on my own. And really, I don't stay in it *all* the time. There's no bathroom in it, you know, but it's my home nonetheless." She put her hand to her forehead and scratched around the outside of the bandage. "This silly thing is going to itch so much."

"Better itching than bleeding." Nico smiled. Some people smiled with only their lips, and maybe their eyes, but when Nico smiled it encompassed his whole face. His startling blue eyes had a lovely twinkle to them, and they drew you in. Well, they drew her in.

Toni shook her head a little, baffled, not wanting to think of the stranger in front of her quite that way, even if he was yummy to look at and smelled like a campfire. Nothing good came from thoughts like that.

"I'll take you to the diner a little way down the block here and call Syn over at the Bear Ridge Inn to prep a room for you. It's the nicest bed and breakfast in town, and it's within walking distance to the diner and the garage."

"That will be handy," she agreed, and then followed him out into the cold to a waiting Jeep. He stowed her bags safely in the back and they drove off. "Where did your dog go?"

"I took her to my mother's house for a bit. I wasn't sure how long you were going to be, or how badly you were hurt. I'll leave her with my mom. I think Jo would shoot me if I brought her into the diner."

"Oh."

"I know, she's a lot cuter and probably more personable than me."

"No, I didn't mean—"

"I'm teasing," he assured her. "So, what do you do?"

"I guess it depends a little on what mood I'm in. Music mostly. Sometimes I take photos or paint pictures or sculpt something. I used to run a little online shop, but it was too annoying trying to keep track of inventory and stuff when I have so little space. What do you do?"

He laughed a little. "It depends. Seriously, take out the music and add in more building and sculpting rather than painting and you've about got it."

"Really? Huh. What do you sculpt with?"

"Sometimes wood, sometimes clay, mostly metal." He pulled into the parking lot in front of an old-fashioned diner that looked straight out of the '50s, all glass, chrome, and vinyl. It was dripping with Christmas decorations, complete with a tree done up in sparkling red, white, and silver in a huge front window. "Jo makes the best pie in town. If we're lucky, she's not out yet."

"We can only hope." Toni unfastened her seat belt.

"Don't move. Let me get the door." He was parked and out of the Jeep before Toni could protest. "This is one of my favorite places."

"Nico. What are you doing here?" A short, pale woman with hair the color of a crow's wing smiled from behind the counter as they walked into the diner, wiping her floured hands off on her red apron. "Oh dear, this must be the girl who had the accident. Are you okay, honey?"

"I'm fine. Or I will be." Toni smiled through gritted teeth, wondering how many people in the tiny town had already heard about her accident. She flushed with embarrassment.

"Doc Cait took care of you, so I'm sure you will be. Let's get you settled and put some food in your belly. Everything is better with food." She grabbed a pair of menus and led them to a booth with deep red vinyl seats and a pristine laminate table top. "I have the perfect thing to start you off. I'll be right back."

"Is everyone so nice here?" Toni asked.

"Yep. It's our specialty."

"Then Bear Ridge must be a special place."

"You have no idea." He smiled.

Jo was back with a broad smile and two mugs of hot chocolate topped with a mound of fluffy white whipped cream with little curls of chocolate hanging on the cream's edges. "Did you figure out what you want?"

"Definitely." Nico smiled as he handed Jo his menu. "I think your herbed meatloaf is exactly what's needed on a night like this."

"Oh, that sounds delicious." Toni's mouth watered at the thought.

"You should know, it's venison, not beef, wrapped in bacon with no egg," Jo explained as she pointed to the listing on the menu.

"No egg?"

"My mom is allergic. I do a lot of cooking without egg."

"I think I'll have the meatloaf as well. He's right. It sounds great." She slid her menu to the edge of the table and sipped at her drink. It was, without a doubt, the most incredible cup of hot chocolate she'd ever had in her life. It might even edge out coffee as her favorite thing ever. Maybe.

"Now, imagine that in pie form." Nico leaned across the table to not quite whisper to her.

"Actually, Nico, tonight is lemon meringue." Jo gestured to the glass-fronted counter where all her hard work was displayed, mounds of perfectly whipped meringue, slightly toasted, like the perfect campfire marshmallow.

"Really?" There was a note of happy surprise in his voice.

"I had an urge." Jo smiled as she walked away. "I had a niggling feeling that you'd be in, and I know it's your favorite."

"I swear to you, her lemon meringue could win prizes all over the world," Nico told Toni with that damnable smile.

Toni stared at him, confused by everything that had happened since she missed hitting the puppy. Everyone was too nice. The town was too perfect. Too cute, too picturesque. It was like something out of a dream she once had. Or a scene from a snow globe. Well, if you took out the part about crashing her dad's truck into a pole.

"So, what's Toni short for?"

"Antoinette, but I prefer Toni."

"I understand, believe me." He laughed. "Nico is not for Nicolas or Nikolai. It's short for Nicodemous."

"I think you said that before. Out at the truck. It's definitely one of those sort of names that's better shortened." She stared at him, unable to stop the smile creeping over her face.

"Yep." He grinned. "My mom was a really big fan of that book, *The Secret of NIMH*, but she didn't want rats."

"Seriously?"

"If I said that my mother has a thing for books, that would be like telling you there is water in the ocean. She's the librarian here in Bear Ridge. All of her children were named after characters in books. I have two older brothers, Grey, for Gandalf the Grey, and Arthur, either for the King or Dent, depending on her mood and if she's had a glass or two of wine. Her dream is for me to name my first-born son Timothy, for the sick mouse kid from the same book."

"At least it's a pretty normal name. Besides, you can make him a hat with horns and a little shirt that says—"

"—There are some who call me... Tim," they said together in a fit of nervous giggles.

"Marry me. Right now, tonight." Nico took Toni's hand in his and pulled it to his heart with exaggerated lash fluttering and stuttering. "A girl who quotes *Monty Python* and didn't ask who Arthur Dent is? That's a woman you keep."

Toni pulled her hand away quickly and was about to form some sort of answer when Jo arrived at the table with two plates of something she might call meatloaf but looked and smelled like no meatloaf Toni had ever seen in her life. It was more like some kind of ultra-gourmet meat cake, dotted with basil and oregano, lines of caramelized onions and mozzarella cheese, all wrapped in thick bacon beside a mound of golden mashed sweet potatoes topped with a dusting of brown sugar. "You shouldn't call this meatloaf. Meatloaf is some sort of mushy oversized baked meatball. This is so not that."

Jo laughed. "I'll take that as a compliment."

"As it's meant to be." Toni stared at her plate almost hesitant to try it, but she tucked in. She was not disappointed, and she was absolutely right that it was like no meatloaf she'd ever had on her lifelong quest for the next pretty place. She and Nico ate in reverent silence, glancing occasionally at each other over the feast before them.

***

When they were done eating, Nico excused himself for a minute and walked over to the counter where Jo was cutting thick slices of pie. Toni watched them, heads leaned slightly together as they whispered about something. The older woman laughed at what Nico said and glanced in Toni's direction with a bright smile.

Toni felt a little pang in her heart watching them. Obviously, they were friends, and close ones from the look of it, but it was only that, friendship. The fact that Nico wasn't romantically involved with Jo was a relief—and that was a new, disconcerting thing to have even thought. Toni made it a point to keep attachments to a minimum with people as well as things. Minimalism in all things, exactly the way her parents had taught her.

Nico walked back to their table with the two plates. He placed a slice of pie in front of her and waited for her to taste it. Toni tried to forget that he was watching her so intently. It was hard to school her expression when the pie was a little piece of bliss. The lemon was tart, the meringue was lightly toasted and fluffy.

"What? Do I have something on my face?" She felt him staring and looked up, pie-laden fork hovering a hair's breadth before her mouth.

"You have an expressive face. I like it. I can tell you're enjoying the pie and I'm glad. There's no better baker in all of Bear Ridge than Jo." He sat down across from her and dug into his slice. "I'll take you to the Bear Ridge Inn when we're done so you can get settled in and then you need to get some rest. How's the head feeling?"

She touched her fingers to the bandage. "Honestly, I'd forgotten about it. Doctor Cait must have the magic touch. It doesn't even feel like it's going to bruise that bad, but I know how hard I hit the wheel. He's got to be a miracle worker."

"Something like that." He shoveled pie into his mouth like he was trying to stop himself from saying more.

Toni looked down at the suddenly empty plate. ""That was flat amazing. I have never in my life had pie like that. You know, I've been in a lot of small towns over the years, but this one—there's something different about it."

"And to think, you've only been in the hospital and the diner so far. Don't worry, we only get stranger from here." He grinned at her.

Toni looked at him for a moment, weighing her options and deciding on her next step. "Where is the cheapest spot to spend a few days here that might have a vacancy?"

"For tonight, your stay is covered over at the Bear Ridge Inn. Tomorrow you can figure out everything else."

"Story of my life." Toni shook her head and sighed. "You're right, though. There's nothing to do but figure it out tomorrow. Well, and hope someone is looking for a spot of help."

"Oh?"

"I'm going to have to stay until the repairs are done, and hotels and food add up to expenses, don't they?" She thought of her locked box and the enormous dent that a prolonged stay in a hotel was going to put in it. She knew the Harvester parts would take a while to find, and even longer to get here. She needed to find a job.

"Tomorrow is soon enough to deal with that."

The silver bells jingled against the glass door and Toni turned her head to watch the biggest, tallest, darkest black man she'd ever seen walk into the diner. She smiled as Jo came around the counter, and the tiny cook launched herself into his arms, then laid a smacking kiss on his lips.

"Her husband?"

"And your mechanic." Nico waved him over when Jo stepped out of his embrace. "Kevin, this is Toni, owner of that truck."

"How're you doing, ma'am? That wasn't a light hit." Kevin extended his hand to her in greeting.

She took it and smiled. Her hand was tiny in comparison. She'd never felt more delicate than in that moment. It was a little weird. "It wasn't, but Doctor Cait seems to have fixed me right up."

The man smiled, his whole face lighting up. "He's the best, for sure. Tomorrow, when you get a chance, come see me so we can talk options. I've never worked on an International Harvester before and I've got to tell you, it's a dream come true. I love the old classics."

"Me too. Especially that one."

"It shows. You've taken excellent care of her."

"Do you think you can actually fix her though?"

"Oh, yes, no problem. I can't promise you the parts will be original, but I can definitely fix her." He sounded confident as he handed her his card. "That's my address there. It's really easy to find."

"She's going to be over at the Bear Ridge Inn," Nico told Kevin.

"Oh, that's super easy. Tomorrow, when you leave the front door of the inn, hang a right, go two blocks and make a left and you'll see the sign."

"Great. Thanks."

"No problem. I'll see you tomorrow. You have a good evening. Toni. Nico." He nodded at them before heading back over to Jo who motioned him to sit before she set his plate up on the counter.

"They're so cute together," Toni said. He makes her look like a little fairy." She watched them for a moment before realizing she was staring.

"Fairies come from fairytales so, that's fitting." Nico smiled at them. "Jo has lived in Bear Ridge all her life, but Kevin is a transplant. He used to do long-haul trucking and one day ended up here."

Jo walked over to them with a bill in her hand. "Are my ears burning?"

"They might be. I was telling Toni here how you and Kevin met."

"That's my favorite story." A wistful look passed over her face. "It was a bit after the lunch rush, so things had calmed down some. He walked in looking tired, but that didn't stop the little pop that went through me. I looked at him and I knew. I saw the man, sure, but really, I saw forever."

Toni felt a rush of warmth. "That might be the sweetest thing I've ever heard in my life."

"Give it time." Jo smiled and glanced quickly at Nico. "One day, you'll know. I was lucky that Kevin felt the same way about me."

"They're the poster children for love at first sight," Nico said, his eyes on Toni, obviously waiting for some kind of response.

Uncomfortable, Toni retreated. "I should really get some sleep."

"No problem." Nico handed some cash to Jo as he scooted out of the booth. He held his hand out to help Toni up, but she didn't take it. "I get that you're not completely sold on me quite yet, and it probably speaks well to your character that you're cautious." He smiled. "I promise, I'll grow on you, if you let me."

Toni followed him out into the snowy evening. It felt so much later than six o'clock, which what her watch said. She shook her wrist to make sure the watch was working. She climbed up into Nico's Jeep and busied herself with her seat belt. They drove in companionable silence down the pretty street. Old buildings in a variety of styles were lit by Christmas lights, and old-fashioned-looking street lamps all decked out in garlands and bows were dotted across the picturesque scenery. One old Queen Anne Victorian drew her eye. She'd always loved that particular style of architecture. It was beautiful, grand, and reminiscent of another time. It made her want to see the inside.

Bear Ridge felt like a place out of time. It felt full of secrets, but not necessarily in a bad way. Like there was a hum underneath everything that spoke to her soul. It felt like magic... as if she had ever believed in magic.

Nico slowed the car, and Toni saw the sign for the hotel. The Bear Ridge Inn was an enormous old mansion, red brick for miles, lit by twinkling white lights along the roof. Battery operated candlesticks were nestled in silver bows, and greenery surrounded each white-trimmed window. Green tin gables peaked up in every direction, capped with chimneys. The deep porch with old-fashioned rockers, and an antique metal glider, looked inviting, like the perfect place to watch a thunderstorm roll through.

"Syn is expecting you. She'll get you settled in, and if you need anything, all you have to do is ask."

"Thanks, Nico."

"It's the least I can do." He smiled as he hopped down out of the Jeep and gathered her things. They didn't even make it to the porch before a lovely woman in her early fifties, with the longest gray-blonde hair Toni had ever seen in her life, stepped out of the house, wreathed in warm light with a welcoming smile.

"Evening, Nico. And you must be Toni."

"I am. And I'm guessing that makes you Syn."

"Nico, take her things on up to the blue room if you would." She reached for Toni's hand.

"No problem." Nico turned to Toni. "I'll see you soon."

"Thanks for dinner. And, um, good night." She resisted the urge to say more as he walked away, not trusting herself to come up with something smart or witty instead of weird. Toni had the feeling she'd see Nico again, but she knew better than to trust those feelings. Nothing was ever guaranteed.

Syn led Toni into the Inn, and crossing the threshold felt a little like stepping into a storybook. A tingle shot up her spine and the hairs on her arms rose. The house smelled of spiced cider, pomanders, and evergreen. Every surface was dusted with holiday cheer. Delicate ceramic figurines, silver menorahs, gourds painted to look like Santa Claus, hand-carved snowmen, and angels of all sorts populated every surface. It looked, felt, and smelled like something straight out of the pages of one of the holiday books she'd read in school as a little girl. The closest she'd gotten to a real Christmas tree was when her family decorated a tree at whatever campground they were parked in for the duration of winter break with popcorn strings and peanut butter-slathered pinecones for the squirrels and birds.

"Welcome to the Bear Ridge Inn." Syn smiled. "We serve breakfast and we have holiday dinners, but this isn't a holiday weekend, so it doesn't really matter today. I hear you've had quite a time of things this afternoon."

"That might be an understatement."

"Well then, let's get you into your room so you can rest. There's nothing so bad that a good soak and a hot fire can't fix it." Syn motioned to the thick leather-bound book that sat open on a podium. "Go ahead and sign the register, if you would."

Toni turned to the book. Pages upon pages of signatures were scrawled on the thick paper, some with a little note about how wonderful their time at the inn had been. She added her name with a flourish. Syn smiled and handed her a shiny new key on a ring with an old-fashioned looking, nearly steampunk-style fob made from an old open barrel key and thick copper wire. "Come on, we'll get you feeling right as rain in no time. I think you'll like the room we've prepared for you."

They walked up the wide grand staircase, and followed the banisters, draped with greenery and tied with red, silver, and gold bows, to a plain door with a modern lock. The door stood open and Toni's luggage was already there, her guitar leaning against the bed beside her duffle. "This is the blue room."

Toni took a long look at the room and was swept up in the magnificence of it. The walls were mostly beautiful cherry bookcases dotted with mirrors, art, and a few spaces where the cream wallpaper showed through. The shelves were covered with books, chunks of pretty stones and Santa Clauses from all over the world. The bedframe was simple, and the bed was piled with pillows in varying shades of blue. A thick down comforter with a pretty blue and white duvet covered the bed. On a low table by the window, a three-foot artificial tree stood, decorated with multicolored lights and antique ornaments in blues and silvers. Toni nearly swooned. She had her own Christmas tree, at least for tonight.

One particular ornament caught her eye. "Is that a spider?" She touched the delicate beaded spider gently. "On a Christmas tree?"

"Can it be that you've never heard the story of the Christmas Spider?" Syn clapped her hands together gleefully. "I love getting to tell this story. Come. Sit down with me."

Syn looked so happy at the chance to tell her tale that Toni couldn't bear to say no, even though she was tired and achy and ready to be by herself for a while. She eyed the antique settee, upholstered in a silver and blue Jacquard and decided that the thick oak framework was more than sturdy enough to hold her.

Syn sat down and angled slightly toward Toni, then cleared her throat and began her story, her melodic voice carrying notes of some faraway place. "A long, long time ago, on a cold Christmas Eve day, a busy mother took her broom to every corner of her house in preparation for the beautiful tree her husband and children had gone to fetch. Her broom sent all the little house spiders fleeing into the attic for the day. One little spider, overcome with excitement for her first Christmas, watched from afar as the family decorated the tree with pretty ornaments.

"That night, long after the family had gone to bed, dreaming of all the treats and goodness in the world, the little spider made her way back downstairs to see the tree. The ornaments twinkled against the green of the perfect tree. The spider was enthralled with the tree and wanted to help make the tree even more beautiful.

"When Santa Claus arrived at the little farmhouse in the woods, the tree was draped in spider silk, artfully arranged by the little weaver in honor of the occasion. Santa Claus being a wise man, and thinking of both the lady of the house and the tiny spider, thanked the young spider sincerely and honored her by turning the threads of silk to silver and gold. The next morning, when the family woke, they were amazed to see the tree shimmering in the morning light, even more beautiful than the night before.

"Now, here in Bear Ridge, to honor the excited little spider, we put one on our tree amidst the strands of silver."

Toni smiled. "I've never heard that story before. It's beautiful."

"It's one of my favorite stories. I always put a pretty little spider on my tree in hopes that she will spin me silver and gold." Syn touched the delicate decoration. "Anyway, I've taken enough of your time.

"The fireplace works and there's enough wood in the bucket at least for tonight. Should you choose to stay longer, we'll bring up more wood. If you need help, all you have to do is ask me or my wife, Vor, and we'll get everything taken care of for you. There are towels and extra toiletries in the closet in the bathroom as well as extra blankets in the cedar chest."

"This is all too amazing." Toni stared openly at her surroundings. "I can't remember ever being in a place that felt so warm and rich. I feel like *The Little Princess*."

"I can't think of a better compliment to receive. Truly." Syn patted Toni's hand and stood. "I should be getting back to work. Oh, the television is inside the armoire. If you get hungry, there's always something good to be had in the kitchen. If you go back down the main stair and go through the archway on the left of the big mirror, that's the dining room. The kitchen is the door at the back of the room. We serve breakfast family style from six to ten a.m."

"Thank you," Toni replied, swallowing a yawn.

"No, thank you. I think—I hope—you'll find the rest you need here." She smiled and set the pretty key down on the table under the tree and walked out of the room.

Toni looked around the room, still in awe of her surroundings. Whatever was going on in the little town, none of it felt real, and certainly not logical. She wished she could say screw it and enjoy the moment—No. This time she wasn't go to shut herself down. She was going to do exactly that, enjoy herself. She'd pay for it. It wouldn't take too big a bite from her nest egg, and she'd hustle extra hard during the summer to make up for one luxurious week or so in this magical little town.

Tonight, she was going to take a long, hot bath in the deepest claw-foot tub she'd ever seen, and sleep in a bed nearly as big as her whole truck.

Chapter Two

Toni woke feeling more rested than she had in a long time, maybe years. Her head didn't hurt. Her neck didn't hurt. For the first time in ages, she didn't want to pull the blanket up over her head for a few more minutes. Instead, she wrapped herself up in a soft alpaca throw and peered out the frosted window. More snow had fallen while she had been sleeping, and it made the whole town look like some great baker in the sky had covered it in sugar. The place looked like it was straight out of a storybook. Which is why Toni didn't—and couldn't—quite trust it.

She dressed in worn jeans and a heavy cable-knit sweater almost the same color blue as the settee in her room. She curled her hair a bit, enough to give it a little shape, and did her makeup. She didn't wear a lot, but she felt a little naked without a little concealer and eyeliner at least.

As she headed down the grand staircase to the dining room, she heard other voices. She couldn't understand what they were saying, but they all sounded happy. When she noticed that the words were punctuated by barking, she couldn't resist moving a tiny bit faster.

All eyes turned to her when she walked into the foyer. She barely registered the people or the Christmas décor she'd missed the night before. She only had eyes for a small, wiggly blur of blue headed in her direction. Toni dropped to the ground at the small pit bull's approach and relished every swipe of its soft tongue, every wiggle, every yip and nip as the dog endeavored to get as close to Toni as her wriggling body could.

"I have to say, I'm a little surprised that you like her, given all the trouble she caused." The gorgeous man who'd come with the dog smiled and Toni's brain stuttered. Nico was dressed in jeans and a plaid shirt, his dark hair brushing the top of his collar. He looked a bit like a lumberjack. Which wasn't a bad thing. "I was dropping off an order down the street and figured I'd stop in and see how you're feeling. From the looks of it, you're doing better."

"I am, thanks. My head doesn't even hurt this morning." She continued to pet the dog who was loving the attention. "I don't know what the doc did, but he must have done something incredible for me not to even have a headache."

"I wish I could take the day and show you around town," Nico said. "Unfortunately, I have a couple of jobs today. Hopefully, you'll have some time for me tomorrow, when I have a whole day open." He took a step toward her and reached out as if he were going to touch her hair but thought better of it. "I like what you've done with your hair."

"Thank you. Though I have to say, you're awfully presumptuous. Maybe I'll have plans tomorrow." She stopped petting Juni, who immediately pawed at her, trying to get her attention.

"I know. It's one of my more annoying qualities. Fortunately, most people think I'm pretty, so it doesn't matter. What about you?"

"Do I think you're pretty? In a Greek lumberjack sort of way, I suppose. 'Pretty' probably isn't exactly the word I'd use."

"Thank you, and I'm Romanian and Greek, but that wasn't what I meant. What's your most annoying quality?" He smiled at her with his perfectly even white teeth, which she tried to conjure as snaggly and discolored. She wanted to put some distance between them in her brain.

"I have no intention of answering that." She stood up and crossed her arms instinctively over her chest.

"That's okay. I'll figure it out myself." He grinned, whistled to the dog, who backed away from Toni, and walked out the door, the bells above it jingling after him.

"I think he's smitten." A tall blonde woman in a heavy black sweater and crisp white apron dusted with flour and sugar laughed. "You must be our newest guest. I'm Vor, Syn's wife. Good morning. I do hope you're a breakfast person. I've made too much again, I think. I've made a mess of frittatas, bacon, sausage, muffins, and Syn has put the coffee on. Or there's water for tea. Come on, dear, the others should be wandering through shortly, if they keep to their own pattern."

"Thank you." Toni followed her into the dining room and stared at the huge table set with thick cream-colored dishes on red and green placemats. Several covered dishes sat on decorative iron trivets down the silver runner that made a shiny river of the center of the table.

"Sit anywhere you like. We've no assigned seating here. We have seventeen guests, now that you're here. Mr. Chalmers won't be down for breakfast. He never gets up before noon. The Taylors will likely be down momentarily." She leaned in conspiratorially. "Try not to sit next to their little boy. He's awfully cute but he never fails to get jam or honey in someone's hair, and it's never his own. Sit, sit. They'll join us when they're ready."

Vor sat at the head of the table and Toni sat in the chair to her right. After reviewing the sumptuous selection, Toni piled her plate high with the most sublime breakfast she'd had in maybe a decade. Then she poured herself a cup of coffee that smelled like angels grew the beans, picked them, roasted them, and brewed them only for her.

"This is all really delicious." Toni couldn't remember the last time she'd enjoyed breakfast this much.

"I'm so glad. It looks like maybe we're a bit early for everyone else still. I have a feeling your day is going to be quite full. I do hope you'll consider staying with us, at least for a few more days."

Toni smiled. She'd love to stay. It was Christmas and it had been years since she'd purposely spent a Christmas somewhere. But she also had an ancient, maybe even antique truck to fix, too. She knew Nico had offered to cover the expenses, but she wouldn't let him even though she'd said she would. The more she had thought about it, the more it bothered her if he paid for the repairs. She had insurance, and her deductible wasn't that high.

"While that would be lovely, I'm going to have to wait and see what it's going to be to fix my truck before I commit."

"I completely understand that. However, I'm also certain we can find a way to make it work for you and us. As you can see, I already cook enough for an army regardless, so what's one more? Currently, we have two other empty rooms, should anyone else show up. You wouldn't be adding any weight to our burden."

It was as if Vor knew exactly the right words to say to ease her mind. "What would the daily rate be?"

"Let me talk it over with Syn and get back to you. I'm sure we can give you quite a reasonable rate, if you're willing to do a few chores."

"And that's something I can definitely work with." A barter-like arrangement was a wonderful idea, and lifted Toni's spirits. Working for something suited her better. She was raised to work for everything she could. "I suppose I'll know more after I talk to the mechanic. He told me how to get there last night, but for the life of me, I can't remember what he said, and the card he gave me wasn't in my pocket."

"Was it Kevin or Bryan who picked up your truck?"

"Kevin."

"Oh, good, he's not far away at all. He'll do right by you. Not that Bryan wouldn't." She dropped her voice to a whisper. "Don't tell anyone, but I like Kevin a tiny bit better."

Toni laughed. "Let me see what the damage there is going to be. Then I'll be able to figure out my plans. I'll stay again tonight either way."

"I'm so glad to hear that." Vor smiled coyly and swept Toni's empty dishes away.

"This place is certainly something," Toni muttered to no one in particular.

"I'm glad you think so." A loud, happy voice startled her. A short, round man in a heavy winter coat appeared in the doorway. "I hear you're new to Bear Ridge. I'm Trevor Gibson, mayor and farmer. Please call me Trevor. It's nice to meet you."

"Um. You too. I'm Toni. Toni Bell." Toni stared at him as he stared at her, his close-set dark eyes looking her over thoroughly.

"I was hoping I could give you a quick little tour of our town." His gaze was sharp, but his tone was light and jovial.

"You're the mayor, huh?" Toni asked, staring at him.

"I am, yes." He bounced a little on the balls of his feet. "I heard about what happened."

"That small-town network, right?" She laughed and shook her head.

"Something like that. It's Christmas time, a hard time to be stuck so far from home, and I thought it was the least I could do to stop by and make sure you have everything you need."

"I get that folks in these little towns are nicer and that news travels ridiculously fast, but I've been in hundreds of little towns and no mayor has ever come to say anything to me before." She took a step back, suddenly uncomfortable with the situation.

"You've never been in Bear Ridge before. Most people who come here end up staying for a while, and do so on purpose. You haven't been given much choice in it. I don't mean to make you uncomfortable or be overwhelming. I don't want to make things worse for you."

"Why are you really here?" She narrowed her eyes at him, feeling like he was purposefully leaving something out.

"Honestly, for a tour. I thought I was being friendly."

She felt a little ashamed at her strange behavior. "I'm sorry. This is all way odd for me. Most places I've been are quite content to let me be another face in the crowd."

"That's sad, Ms. Bell."

"This town is beautiful, though a little too friendly maybe. It's like something straight out of a holiday movie—and I wasn't looking to have any sort of a role in anyone's winter play."

Trevor laughed. "I'll make sure to take that off the itinerary."

Toni smiled awkwardly at his joke that didn't actually feel like a joke, and considered him and her next words carefully. "Am I dead?"

Trevor started laughing. Not a giggle, not a chuckle, but a deep, belly-laughing guffaw. "No. I assure you, you are very much alive. Bear Ridge is a lot of things, but it is neither Heaven, nor Hell, or even Limbo. Even with that accident, I don't think you were ever in danger of dying."

"There *is* something weird going on. I'm not wrong about that."

"No, you're not wrong exactly. It's nothing nefarious or bad. Bear Ridge is not a normal place, you're right, and perceptive. Like I said, we don't get a lot of visitors. And that's what makes it all so interesting." He shifted in his coat. "Would you be willing to come with me? Let me show you some of the town? I promise to try to not be too friendly." He grinned.

Toni paused. He seemed genuine enough, if a little odd. Maybe it had really been that long since the last time people were more than superficially polite. Despite her wariness, her curiosity was always going to get the better of her in the end anyway. "What if, instead of a tour, you accompany me on my walk instead. No special treatment, only a bit of company while I explore a new place."

"I think that would be lovely." He smiled brightly.

"Great. Let me get my coat."

On the way back to her room to get her coat, she passed an older couple on the staircase as they made their way to breakfast. They smiled at her but didn't really see her. The man was whispering something in the woman's ear that made her blush and giggle and Toni felt like she was intruding on a special and private moment. She grabbed her coat and purse and locked up the door before making her way back to the mayor. "All right. I'm ready."

"Good." He led her out into the quite cold but beautiful day. Everything was decorated for the holidays—every lamp post, every house, every business. The decorations weren't overdone. They were beautiful. Some of them were childish and cartoony and others were traditional with old-world charm. All of the winter holidays seemed to be represented, old and new: Christmas, Solstice, Yule, Kwanzaa, St. Lucia Day, Chanukah, and probably some she didn't know. If she could have designed a perfect Christmas picture for a card, this is what it would be. All of the winter holidays, all of the styles, all of the joy, inclusive. Perfect.

"You really love Christmas here."

"Doesn't everyone?" Every word he said either sounded happy or confused or both. "If you look to your left, that first street there, it was the first real street in all of Bear Ridge. It used to be cobblestone, but we had a few too many complaints about the noise when the big trucks started coming through regularly. A lot of our smaller streets are still cobbled though."

"Interesting." Toni didn't know what else to say.

"Not really. It's very nice of you to say so though." He pointed to the right. "About six blocks that way you'll find the town square. We have a lot of little events and such in the big gazebo there. Not every city uses their square for proper meeting space anymore."

"I wouldn't know, to be honest. I don't think I've ever been to any town meeting."

"Maybe if you're here long enough, you could see what one is like." He thought for a moment. "There's a caroling event next week; you should come."

"I'll think about it." She turned at the corner and headed for the beautiful Queen Anne Victorian that had caught her eye even in the dark the night before. In the light of day, it was even more beautiful. The steely blue siding was offset by the pristine white trim and accented with the occasional furl and swirl of wrought-iron filigree.

"I do hope you'll come. It's a wonderful time, and someone said you were a musician of some kind."

"I dabble a little." Toni couldn't help it; the more time she spent with him, the more she liked him. He was a silly little man who didn't seem to realize how much his enthusiasm came off as awkward.

As she approached the Victorian house, she realized it wasn't only a house. There was a sign painted to match the siding hanging from a wrought-iron spiral beside the ornate front door that read, "Past Presents and Futures Told," in bold gold script, and a red and white sign, it said "Open" in the bay window. A raven sat on top of the sign. Toni thought it was stuffed until she passed by it and it made a low strange sound as if water was dripping fast into a copper pot. She looked at it strangely, noting that the mayor hadn't seemed the least bit surprised by the sound. Maybe she'd never heard a raven's call properly before.

There were no bright jingling bells as the door opened, but it didn't matter. The moment Toni stepped onto the mat in front of the door, a woman swept into the foyer. She didn't step or walk—she absolutely glided, no feet in sight beneath the hem of her long skirt that brushed the ground with a whisper, and not a single clop of a heel or creak of a board. She had one of the most interesting faces Toni had ever seen. There was no way to determine her age. She looked simultaneously young and ancient. When Toni looked directly at her she seemed interesting enough, but when she saw her in her periphery, she was the most beautiful woman Toni had ever seen in her life. Her entire figure was wreathed in purple wispy smoke that shifted and gathered to stay close when she walked.

"You can call me Max." The woman held her hand out to Toni, who took it. The woman deftly flipped her hand so that it was palm up and took a long look at it. "Hm."

"What are you doing?" Toni didn't snatch back her hand or object, since she found herself deeply interested in whatever was happening. Where Max's thin and cool skin touched hers, it was like electricity dancing on her flesh.

"Taking your measure. Though, how I am to figure you out when you haven't figured *you* out yet is beyond me."

"You have a lovely house." Toni blurted the first thing that came to her mind, nervous energy bubbling up and babbling out. She didn't look at anything except the woman in front of her, almost afraid to look away.

"Thank you. You have a lovely soul." She looked into Toni's eyes with lingering grief and let her hand go. "You've had a time of it, haven't you?"

Toni nodded without thinking, without hesitating. As soon as she noticed herself behaving strangely, she put her guard up a bit. She decided to try and take hold of the conversation in self-defense. "Do you live here too?"

Max nodded. "I live upstairs. That's not really what you want to know, though. You have a lot of questions. Why don't you come and sit with me? We'll have a cup of tea and I'll tell you a story. Maybe it will answer some of them."

Toni turned to Trevor, who was taking off his overcoat and hanging it on the tall wooden rack beside the door. "I'll take care of your coat, if you wish," he said.

Toni slipped out of her coat and walked quickly to catch up to the woman in purple before her house swallowed her up completely. Everything the woman wore was some shade of purple. Even her shoulder-length hair, though it was dark, held notes of purples from plum to blackberry.

Max led Toni through the house, out of the front rooms and into a glassed-in solarium off the kitchen. There were plants everywhere, only a few of which Toni could identify. It smelled like summer in the middle of winter. A small fountain bubbled over pretty polished spheres of quartz and amethyst down into a pool that held a single golden koi.

Max sat down at a glass-topped iron table already set for tea and motioned for Toni to join her. She began speaking as she poured, and her melodic voice carried a hint of Scotland in it, as if she'd left it behind her many years before. "I think you've noticed, but Bear Ridge is not like other little towns. In fact, it may not be like any other town in the world. Many pass through, sometimes stopping for a meal or to shop or because they've come to find something specific. Most leave, heading back to their lives, and never think of us again. We are the prettiest, most magical little town that no one can remember."

"What?" Toni sniffed at the tea; it was heavy on the apple and smoky flavors. She added a little honey instead of sugar and stirred. The words Max was saying were clearly in English, but something, somewhere must have been lost in translation.

"I understand your doubt, but I promise I fully understand the words that I use, that you hear. This town has been around for an incredibly long time—no one knows how long. Technically, we aren't exactly sure where we are, because the roads come from everywhere. Those of us who have lived here for a long time, we've learned what history we can, we've parsed together a bit more, and we still don't know as much as we'd like. Most people really are simply passing through. Usually, they're looking for something, a direction or a thing, and often Bear Ridge gives them what they most need." Max sipped at her own tea and looked into Toni's eyes. "You have been lost for a long time. You have dealt with great loss. It has marked you. You have been through many trials and come through them stronger for it."

"That's true of everyone." Toni felt her defensiveness rising.

"You're right. More or less." Max opened the wooden box on the table and plucked out a deck of large cards with a purple-hued wheel on the back.

"I don't really believe in that sort of thing."

"Oh?" Max laughed a sort of well-meaning bless-your-heart sort of laugh. "My cards don't need you to believe at all."

She laid three cards face down on the table and covered them with her hands. Toni rolled her eyes but made no move to stop Max as she flipped the cards over. "I know you're having a hard time with all of this, everything going on. You've been drawn here for a reason. You feel that, even if you don't want to admit it. You will struggle against it; however, I believe you are on the cusp of a great revelation."

"That's patently ridiculous." Her tone was light, even cheerful, but the notes rang false.

"You are now the page of Wands, full of brilliance and excitement. You have held on to your freedom like it was your only possession. This ace of Swords tells me that you are about to find some clarity, that the way will be made clear for you to become the woman, the artist, that you are meant to be."

"And you think I'm going to find all of this here and become"— she glanced at the third card—"an Empress? What the hell does that even mean?"

"Nothing you don't already know deep down inside yourself but you're too damned afraid to look."

"What happens when I leave Bear Ridge? Can I leave it?"

Max looked disgusted and annoyed. "Of course. You're no prisoner. You can leave whenever you wish. No one will ever keep you against your will here. As best we can tell, when you leave, you will forget this town, this place, the time you spent here."

"Why is everyone so nice? Why do they want me to stick around?" Toni wished she had a flashlight or a spotlight to better interrogate Max, who was definitely keeping something from her.

"What? You'd rather we were terrible? You'd like us to do terrible things? Maybe tie you up and sacrifice you to one of the older gods?" She rolled her eyes in exasperation.

Toni thought her word choice was rather odd but that led to a door that she had no intention of opening any time soon.

"I wish I had words that you could hear right now. There is too much fog in your heart to hear what needs to be said. I don't think you're going to be receptive to anything more I have to say today. I hope you'll come back to see me when things are a little clearer." Max stood up and left the room in a swirl of whispering purple without another word, leaving Toni sitting alone in her beautiful garden.

Toni finished her tea, set down the cup and glanced in the bottom of it. "Hopefully a star is a good thing," she said to herself.

"It means good luck," Max yelled from nowhere.

Toni picked up her purse and walked quickly back to the front room where Trevor was still waiting for her, leaning over the glass display cases to peer at their contents. He looked up at her with concern on his face. "Are you all right?"

"I don't know. Sorry. I don't do mumbo-jumbo and that's all you have for me. I'm sorry, Mr. Mayor, but I think I'm going to cut our walk short and go find out about my truck. I'm thinking the faster I get out of this crazy place, the better off I'll be."

"Should you need anything, you can find me out at my farm. Anyone can tell you how to get there." He looked sad, even offended.

"Did you come into town for the express purpose of meeting me?" She felt emotions bubbling up inside her. "None of this is in any way normal."

"I really don't like it when people are mad at me." Trevor's face drooped, the lines deepening. "You've had a stressful day and I don't want to make it worse, so I'm going to go now. If you want to talk or have questions for me, I'm easy to find. I hope I'll see you again before Christmas. Please have a good day." He smiled at her again as he gathered himself into his coat and headed out into the extremely cold day.

"Are you kidding me?" She asked the empty room, aggravated with everyone, even herself. She didn't know what they had to gain playing their little parlor-trick games, but it couldn't be good, and she was done with all of it. Toni took a deep breath before bundling up. She caught a glimpse of herself in a large, ornate mirror. She looked annoyed. And too pale. However, the circles under her eyes were lighter than they had been earlier that morning.

Like Max wore a strange cloud of purple, Toni also wore a cloak of misted color, only hers was thin and gray and rather ugly. It didn't really suit her well at all.

When she stepped out of the beautiful old house, everything in Bear Ridge felt a little less fantastic, a little tarnished. Now, she was cold and maybe a bit angry as she trudged through the beautiful town searching for her truck, for her life, for the next step. Anything.

She felt eyes on her, noticed the quivering curtains, but never saw the faces behind them. She understood that it was a small town, but it was touristy enough that her presence should barely have twitched the whiskers of the local gossip. A ringing bell caught her ear. Maybe the place wasn't that far out of reality if there was still a Santa standing on a corner ringing a bell.

"Are you all right, ma'am?" he asked.

"Ma'am? Do I look so old?" She sighed.

"No. You do look sad today, though. It's a terrible time of year to be sad." He set his silver bell in the gold bucket and stepped toward her, arms open.

"Well, Santa, you'd be sad too, in my position. And maybe a little annoyed or angry or confused." She stepped away from the coming hug fast enough to stop it before it started.

"It sounds like you're having a really rough day." His smile was kind and his full white beard looked real, matching the short white curl that lay on his forehead, jutting from under the fur-trimmed red cap.

"You don't know the half of it." She clasped her fingers together and blew on them.

"Come, let's sit down and you can tell me all about it."

"Oh, please, like you don't know already. You're from this crazy place where everyone knows everything, and apparently I'm the topic of everyone's conversation."

"I'm sorry to hear that. Usually Bear Ridge is nothing but warm and friendly." His stormy gray eyes lost their twinkle for a moment and he looked honestly upset that she was having difficulties.

"Oh, it's warm and friendly," she agreed. "It's also nosy and weird and too much. The freaking mayor came to meet me for goodness sake."

Santa looked at her strangely as he subtly guided her to the bench to sit down. "Trevor gets a little over excited when it looks like someone interesting might stay for more than a day. Honestly, no one can hold it against him since no one can remember his behavior once they leave here. Most people find him charming, maybe a bit weird, but mostly they leave in a day or two, so what's the harm?"

"And everyone who stays longer stays forever, right?"

"What? No. That's not how any of it works." Santa laughed. "I think I understand a little better why you look like someone has sentenced you to some dark prison somewhere. I think maybe you've misunderstood a few things. No one expects you to stay."

She looked at him and decided to go with it. Everyone else was crazy, what was one more ridiculous person? None of it could really be happening anyway. Any minute she was going to wake up in some hospital bed somewhere after the most incredibly involved hallucination ever. "The terrible thing is, I'd love to stay here for a bit, even if I *did* have a choice. It's beautiful here. It's been a long time since I spent Christmas in a place that actually felt and looked like Christmas should."

"I know." Santa smiled knowingly, his blue eyes twinkling.

"Right, because you're Santa," she scoffed.

"And you haven't believed in anything since you were eight. No gods, no fairies, no magic, no happily-ever-afters."

"Maybe there is magic, but it's not for me. Magic belongs in places like this where people pass through, find a little of what they need, and move on."

"Interesting." He sounded like a therapist whose patient was on the brink of a revelation.

"What?"

"Nothing really. You sound like someone who *does* believe in a lot of things—in this place, in these people, maybe even me, deep down enough." Santa took her hands in his. "Tell me what you want for Christmas, Toni."

She swallowed hard, stared into the face of what could only be a madman and found herself confessing her deepest wishes. Had she told him her name? Had he heard it from some nosy gossip? "All I really want is to know what I want. I know that doesn't make sense to you. But, I do really want to know."

"On the contrary. It makes perfect sense." Santa smiled as he released her hands and stood. "I can't make you any promises, but we'll see what I can do."

She was about to respond—her mouth was getting ready to move—but she blinked and he was already gone as if he'd never been there at all. Not even bootprints in the snow where she knew he'd been ringing his bell. She saw him. She heard him. He had held her hands in his and comforted her. He really had been there, solid as the bench she was sitting on, warm and alive.

Toni shook her head and looked around. There was no one on the street at all, let alone a bell-ringing Santa. It was true, Bear Ridge was a beautiful little town. Beautiful and strange. If it wasn't a hallucination, maybe she was going insane... maybe she'd been alone too long.

She was standing in front of a cute little park complete with a child's playground that was probably filled to bursting in the summers, and was edged by hedgerows that likely flowered in the spring. In the center of the park was a little gazebo draped in festive bunting. A covered community board beside the gate had a calendar of events and several flyers. The calendar was full of Christmas and holiday things: a few tree lightings and a parade on dates that had already passed, but the community caroling was coming up in a few days. Two craft fairs, one at a school and one at a church. A pot luck dinner at the lodge. A toy drive. A meal delivery service for the elderly, pregnant, and ill. And a community party with a tree, ending with the crowning of queens. It was a town full of wonderful and extraordinary things.

So why did she want to leave so badly?

She tried to use her phone to get directions, but her service was terrible in Bear Ridge. She saw they had a tower—its light blinked at night—so it didn't make much sense that her phone wasn't pinging right, but nothing was cooperating with her anymore. Frustrated, she headed for the little tea shop a few buildings down. "Teas Me" had a gray stone front trimmed in cotton candy pink with windows full of Christmas tea sets and sugary looking cakes.

"Good morning." The woman behind the counter was soft and cheerful. Her dark earthy skin was ridged and lined with years of laughter, her gray hair coiling like soft springs in every direction. She wiped her flour-dusted hands off on her crisp green apron and appraised Toni. "You look more like a coffee drinker than a tea drinker."

"You're not wrong. Sorry." She held up her hands in surrender and the woman laughed.

"Ha. Nothing to be sorry about, darlin'. You'll get no judgment here. I do, in fact, enjoy, make, and carry both. Have seat, have a cup, warm up."

"If you're going to twist my arm, I think a little cup might be nice." Toni smiled and shrugged out of her coat and sat down at a small, delicate-looking table.

"Here you go." The proprietress set a pretty mug swirled with purple, blue, and silver in front of Toni, steam curling up from the top.

Toni inhaled, pulling the scents of coffee both roasted and brewed expertly with a slight hint of cinnamon. "Thank you. This is perfect."

"Cream or sugar?"

"No thanks."

"Really?" The ancient woman's black eyes sparked with an intense intelligence.

"My parents drank theirs black, and I learned to do the same when there was no cream or sugar or honey in the truck." Toni took a sip and immediately felt a little better. "Maybe you can help me. I'm looking for a garage. I know the guy with the tow truck's name is Kevin and he's married to the lady at the diner, but I completely forgot all the rest of what he told me."

The woman laughed. "No problem at all. You were almost there. If you'd gone to the end of this block, you wouldn't have missed it. Especially since it's called Kevin's Garage."

"Yeah, that'd be the one." Toni shook her head, feeling a little bit stupid, and took another sip of the magic coffee. "Thanks."

"No problem. Can I get you anything else?"

"Um." She gave it some thought. "Not today. I know I'll be back. It's going to take a miracle to get my truck fixed before Christmas."

"I'm sorry to hear that, dear. Were you on the way home?" Her voice was rich and slow like warm molasses.

"Oh no, I've got nowhere better to be. No one left to be there with." The words came out before she realized how telling they were. There was something about this place, these people, that opened her all the way up like she had no secrets. She didn't like it at all. It had happened before in the antiques and fortunes shop and again with the disappearing Santa, and it gave her the creeps.

"I'm quite sure you're wrong about that. Everyone has someone, even if they don't realize it." She smiled sweetly and went back behind the counter, getting back to kneading her dough.

Toni finished her coffee and debated getting another cup to go. She didn't even get the chance to decide before the woman handed her a cup.

"Thank you." Toni wrapped her hands gratefully around the heavy paper cup.

"You look like you need it."

"I'll see you again tomorrow, for sure." She searched for a nametag.

"Nope. No tags here. No one uses my real name anyway. Everyone around here calls me Nana." She smiled, her dark eyes shining with an eerie inner light. "I'll see you tomorrow. Maybe I'll even make you something special."

"Don't go to any trouble on my account."

"Now, honey, I think it's been too long since anyone did, don't you?" Nana kept waving until Toni was out of sight of the windows.

***

Nana had given her perfect directions. Kevin's Garage was exactly where she said it was and her day was looking up immensely. It wasn't going to be half as horrible as she feared to fix the Harvester. International Harvester parts were not easy to come by and she needed a new radiator, a new fan, and a new front panel. Fortunately, Kevin was a well-connected mechanical genius and had a line on both a panel and a radiator out of two junkyards. She would have to retire the truck eventually. She had always hoped it would last until she finally settled down. In the best news of the day, the camper top hadn't been damaged at all. That would have been a nightmare to try and fix.

Her favorite childhood memories were all tied up in that truck, that camper. Traveling from beach to beach every weekend, every vacation, even a few sick days here and there. It was why she'd never been able to have pets growing up. Pets meant more responsibility, less camping, less surfing, less climbing, less hiking. At least the neighbor who had taken her in for a few years after her parents died had been happy to let her store the truck in his barn until she graduated high school. Now she was an adult, Uncle Gabby was dead too, and she was living the life her mother had longed for, always on the move, never in one place for long.

She'd been on the road for nearly seven years, going from town to town, living mostly off the proceeds from selling Uncle Gabby's farm and what her parents left behind. Sometimes, when she was bored or wanted to pad the liner again, she would set out her case and play, or pick up a steadier gig until it was time to move on. She lived about half the time out of her truck and the other out of motel rooms. If not for bathrooms with tubs and showers, she'd always live out of her truck, but solar showers sucked, more so for a woman with long hair who was not a big fan of dry shampoo and had a great love for her curling iron.

With an estimate of nearly a grand for repairs, she was considering finding some short-term work on top of doing whatever chores Vor and Syn had for her. However, if she didn't find something it wouldn't be the worst thing. She could cover it. She hated dipping too much into her safety net, but money could be replaced with a little determination and creativity. She'd figure it out. She always did.

Toni took a few minutes to climb up into the back of the Harvester and get the rest of what she needed to get by until the truck was finished. She didn't want to keep bothering Kevin while he was working on putting her home back together. Surprisingly, she wasn't the least bit worried about the safety of the few things she did have while her truck sat alone in Kevin's lot. In the light of day, the damage was both worse and better than she'd expected; the actual damage was worse than she'd thought, but it didn't hurt her heart as bad as she'd expected—and that was better.

As she walked back toward the inn, the sound of hammering caught her ear. It seemed a little cold for any sort of construction work. The closer she got to the inn, the closer the sound was. She turned the corner onto the main thoroughfare and spotted Nico. It looked like he was building something out of metal in the front yard of the beautiful Queen Anne that housed the little witchy shop run by the crazy tarot lady, Max.

"You get an estimate on your truck?" He called to her, motioning her closer. He was assembling some strange metal sculpture.

"I did. For the work and all. It turns out your mechanic is a pretty decent guy."

"Tell me something I don't know." He smiled, obviously genuinely glad. "I'd like to help cover that, if you'll let me."

"I appreciate that, I do. I don't need you to do that." She shook her head. "Actually, I'd rather you didn't. I'm perfectly capable of taking care of my own."

"Wasn't saying that you weren't." He wiped his hands off on a towel and stepped even closer. "You're beautiful when you're annoyed with me."

"And you're better than such a lame line."

"Let me see if I can do better then. Your eyes sparkle like cut peridots and your hair shines like a sunrise." He put his hand to his forehead and mock-swooned. "You must be a broom, because you swept me off my feet."

"Yeah. No. That was so much worse." Toni turned to hide her uncontrollable grin and pointedly looked at the metal in the yard, the pieces scattered on the snow. They were preassembled pieces that needed to be put together. In a pile of pieces as they were, she could not tell what it was supposed to be. "Isn't it a little cold to be working with metal?"

"You'd think so, but no, not really. I put the base in before the freeze." He motioned to the large rock with a long piece of rebar sticking up out of it. "I put the rest of it together in my shop before bringing it out. If you come back around this way in two or three hours, you'll be able to tell what it is. Actually no, come back in four hours and get to see the finished product. Then you can take me out to dinner."

"What if I had plans already?" she asked. His confidence both intrigued and irritated her. He really was interesting and not terrible to look at either. Plus, she really was curious what the pile of scrap could be.

He clutched at his chest. "You wound me, madam. No, seriously, come back and see her when she's finished. I promise it'll be worth it."

Toni stared at the pieces and could not see what they could be. She decided that just this once, she wanted to know enough to bend her personal rules about really cute men that looked like husband and father material. "All right, fine. I'll come look at this pile of metal, but I'm not promising dinner."

"How about this…" He stepped toward her. "If it wasn't worth coming back for, you can find your own dinner. If it was, you'll trust me to find the best dinner in all of Bear Ridge."

"That isn't at your own house."

Nico sighed and held up his hand as if taking an oath. "Fine. That isn't at my own house."

"It's a deal." She held out her hand to shake.

Nico raised his eyebrows and looked at her hand for a moment before taking it. "I should warn you that I am a terrible cook beyond frozen stuff that comes already made. If I'm promising you good food, it won't be at my house. For the record."

"I merely want to make sure that the terms are understood at the outset." She looked away to hide the blush that crept over her face.

"I should get back to work if I'm going to have this built in four hours." He walked back to the stone and settled a piece of metal down over the post. He wrapped a black bandana over his hair before shoving the welding mask on over it.

Toni wanted to watch without being creepy and staring at him. She'd have to be blind not to notice how nicely he filled out his jeans or how wide his shoulders were. If the blue-eyed, dark-haired look happened to be her thing, that wasn't because of him; it had always been that way. Nico happened to check off many of her personal preference boxes... but that didn't mean anything. Dinner wasn't anything important, it was a meal they both needed to eat. For the second night in a row. That didn't mean anything either. At least this time she wasn't concussed.

She touched her head, amazed at the difference a night made. She had never been in an accident like that before, but she was pretty sure gashes and concussions didn't go away overnight. The doctor was either exceptionally good or it hadn't been nearly as bad as she'd thought. She hadn't even had to take any of the pills he'd given her for pain.

As Toni made her way back to the inn, she noted the little kids playing in the snow, building snowmen, making snow angels, sledding down small hills. They were watched and sometimes even joined by happy, laughing parents, sometimes a dog in the yard or a cat in the window. Happiness oozed from them on that pretty Tuesday afternoon, right at the beginning of the grand countdown to Christmas. Jealousy perched on her shoulder, but she quieted it easily enough. She'd had most all the childhood moments any kid could hope for.

She found a list of light chores waiting on her made bed. For the amount of the discount they were proposing to give her, it was definitely weighted in her favor. She figured she would do a little extra because they were so kind to her. And it really was a beautiful inn. Once upon a time, it had been an extraordinary house, she could tell. It probably started its life as a luxurious colonial mansion in the 1850s, with at least one wing added to the back—maybe two. Toni glanced at the clock and figured she had about three hours before she was supposed to go back to see what Nico was building, and she could absolutely get the shared spaces dusted and vacuumed, no problem.

Vor had given her directions on how to find the rags, cleaners, and vacuum, and what rooms needed what done. She loaded up her music, shoved her headphones on, and got to work. Toni took pride in her work and did the best job she could, but it didn't take up the entire three hours. So, she took a hot bath, soaking and daydreaming until her fingers went pruny.

She dressed and took some care with her hair and makeup. It wasn't exactly stage ready, but it was close to her happy place with mostly purples and silvers. Her mother always told her that purple shades brought out the golden flecks in her green eyes and she liked the way it turned out. Her stage look was a little more hippie-glam with a healthy dose of pixie dust and sparkle, flowy skirts and dresses in shades of gray and blue with crazy splashes of purple and silver. It was cold enough that she wore velvet leggings under her long, dark purple skirt.

"Don't you look lovely." Syn wolf-whistled as Toni came down the stairs.

Toni couldn't help the deep blush that spread across her whole self. "Thanks."

"Going somewhere special?"

"I don't exactly know." She laughed and shook her head. "Part of me thinks this whole thing is crazy and I should hole up in my room until my truck is ready and get the hell out of dodge while I can."

"And the other part of you?"

"That part of me is a lunatic who isn't speaking to me right now. I don't exactly know what she's thinking but it sure as hell isn't about running away." Her voice went soft and whimsical and Toni shut her mouth hard to keep anything else from coming to light.

"Isn't that interesting?" Syn took a few steps toward her and laid her hands lightly on Toni's shoulders. "I know we're a bit much and we come on a little strong—we as a whole, not me specifically, of course."

"Of course." Toni grinned along with her.

"Really though, I know you're struggling with this place, and I wish you weren't."

"Me too. I'm not used to having so many people wanting to be part of the conversation. There have been times when I've gone weeks without talking to anyone at all. I think I'm a bit overwhelmed by your friendliness, if that makes sense." Toni found herself being more honest than she'd intended. She had to get better at keeping her words in her head. She smiled, pulled her coat on, and headed out into the darkening afternoon, ready to see a man about a pile of metal.

The moment the yard came into view, Toni knew she'd lost. And she knew he knew it. What he'd put together from a pile of bits and bobs and gears and various pieces of repurposed sheet metal, was nothing short of a miracle. The dragon stood nearly as tall as her, solar lights in its eyes, sparking a glow behind the frosted blue-green glass. She stared openly at it for a minute before the artist himself came bounding out the shop door, cleaner and fresher than Toni'd expected.

"Max let me wash up when I finished," he explained with a cheeky grin.

"You're an incredible artist."

"Thank you." He smiled, accepting the compliment without argument. "Worth coming all the way back here in the cold?"

"You knew it would be." She smiled at him. "Did you know that dragons are my favorite mythical creature?"

"I did not. Now that I do, I won't forget." He took her hand in his and they both jumped at the bright spark that snapped between their hands when their flesh touched. "I hope you're hungry."

"Actually—" She paused for a second, fully intending to back out, to make her excuses, but her mouth had other plans. "I'm starving."

"Great. For a minute there, I thought you'd back out."

"Me too." She resigned herself to the evening and hoped it wasn't a mistake.

"I like an honest woman." He laughed. "Come on, it's not too far."

He helped her up into his truck and she asked, "Where are we going?"

"The diner is great, and I love it—and Jo really does make the best pie maybe anywhere, but we also have the best Greek restaurant anywhere in the world."

"Even Greece?"

"Maybe even so." Nico smiled broadly but the smile fell quickly. "I hope you like Greek food."

Toni patted his hand as he climbed up beside her, noting her desire to keep touching him and trying hard to quash it. "You're in luck. I happen to love spanakopita."

Relief was obvious on his face as he started up his truck and eased into the snowy street. They passed a number of pretty houses and brightly lit businesses. When they reached the actual heart of Bear Ridge, the difference was startling. It was busier than Toni would have expected, people walking down the sidewalk with bags and packages, all bundled up against the cold. Parents gripping tiny hands shoved in thick woolen mittens, adjusting brightly colored scarves against wind-reddened cheeks with a smile and shining eyes brought on a sense of helpless nostalgia that made her ache for her own long-lost family. It was enough to make a grown woman get a little weepy and retrospective. It was everything right about the world in one little place.

Nico pulled his truck into one of the few open spots on the street. "It's not too far from here—are you okay to walk a block or two?"

"I'm not the one that spent all day welding metal. I'm fine." She laughed and zipped up her coat.

"You're going to want this." Nico reached behind the seat and pulled up a pair of scarves, one blue and one red and white checked. "I hate to cover your pretty face, but it really is cold tonight."

"Thank you." Toni wrapped the blue length of soft fleece around her throat and pulled her cap down over her ears. The fabric smelled like him, all wood smoke and sweat, and she didn't want to give it back.

Nico tried to reach the door to help her out, but Toni beat him to the punch, hopping lightly down out of the cab before promptly slipping a little on a small patch of ice. Fortunately, Nico was close enough for Toni to grab his arm to steady herself. She was met with a grin, and she rolled her eyes at him, a little aggravated at how much steadier she felt with her arm tucked securely into his as they walked down the street.

They heard the sound of reedy pipes playing along with a bright violin, their Celtic-sounding rendition of "I Saw Three Ships" almost enough to make even Toni want to dance a little. Her fingers couldn't help but tap on Nico's arm as she instinctively strummed the guitar accompaniment. It was a beautiful, happy arrangement.

"You're a musician, right?"

Toni shrugged. "Sure."

"I'd love to hear you play sometime."

"I'll email you my next concert date." She laughed before noticing the slight frown on Nico's face and the sadness in his eyes. She didn't want to be the cause of that sadness. "What? What did I say?"

"It's not important." Nico pasted his smiled back on his face and held open the door for her.

The restaurant was lovely, light, bright, and beachy with pops of brilliant blues and sandy-colored walls dotted with old clay olive jars and marble statuary. It felt inviting and smelled like sweet herbs and grape leaves. The exuberant young hostess sat them at a small table in front of the window, giving them pretty menus and a recommendation for the baklava cheesecake. Toni lost herself for a moment in the menu, somewhere between a gyro platter and the pastitsio.

"She's not wrong about the cheesecake. I'd save room for it." Nico smiled at her and set his menu down.

"There is always room for cheesecake. I'm not sure I've ever had baklava cheesecake before, though." She continued to look at the menu but wasn't really seeing words anymore. She knew what she wanted anyway. Any good Greek place could be judged on two things, their spanakopita and moussaka, at least when going to a lovely dinner. For lunch, she'd have ordered the gyro instead.

"What are your plans while you're sort of stuck here?" he asked her after they'd ordered.

"I don't know exactly. I'll be doing some light housekeeping for the inn to cut my costs a little, but other than that, I haven't thought that far ahead."

"What would you be doing if you weren't in Bear Ridge, then?"

"Driving." She laughed, slightly surprised by her honesty. "I didn't really have plans."

"What about family?"

"I don't actually have any." She glanced up at him and realized that he expected more of an answer than that. "Yeah, you and me? We're not there yet."

Nico pursed his lips and nodded. "I like that word—yet."

Toni rolled her eyes. "You don't know me."

"You're right. I don't. You could be a horrible musician, or worse, a hoarder." He smiled at her, reaching over the table to take her hand in his. "I'm about to be perfectly honest with you, Toni. I'm even going to be serious for a minute here. I know you think I'm nuts, that this place is nuts, the whole shebang. I get that. I look at you and I see something that could be forever."

"Could be?"

"I learned a long time ago that just because something feels like it could be something for one person, it doesn't mean that the other person sees the same kind of potential."

"So, you've seen forever before?" For some reason, the idea of that made Toni's heart a little heavy—which made no sense because she had no interest in forever in the first place.

"Not for me. I watched my older brother come to understand that what looks like forever to one person might look like a fun evening to another." He shrugged. "I was young and stupid and took it all to heart. Don't worry about him though, he found a different vision of forever and we all think she suits him better. I understand that some things aren't meant to be the way we might want them to be. I see possibilities for us—and maybe I'm under that same delusion my brother was, but if I don't take half a chance, I'll always wonder."

Before Toni could find the words to respond to that, the appetizers arrived, and she was lost to the world of spinach and cheese. Dinner was, without a doubt, some of the best Greek food Toni had ever had, and the company wasn't bad either, even if he did tie her up in knots. They explored topics that many wouldn't on a first date, like religion (eclectic and sporadic at best) and politics (mixed bag), and favorite bands (Juliette and the Licks and Stevie Nicks for her, Metallica and the Ramones for him). For many, these were make-or-break conversations that were far more likely for the end of relationships. The last time Toni had a conversation reaching that far into what matters, she was still in high school and lived in a real house with a foundation and acreage… during the week at least.

At the end of the dinner, Toni knew two things: she really liked Nico and she really didn't want to. When he pulled up in front of the inn, Toni said a hurried goodnight and instead of leaning in like he so obviously wanted her to, she bolted for the safety of her room without looking back, far away from Nico and his beautiful, kissable mouth. Far away from everything that wasn't part of how she envisioned her future.

Chapter Three

Toni stared at the smooth plaster ceiling, wishing she hadn't gone with her cowardice and fled from the lips that wanted to kiss her, the hands that wanted to explore. Sleep hadn't gone well at all with images of Nico dancing in her head. He wasn't the sort of boy a girl could walk away from, and she wasn't the sort of girl who stayed. She was living for three; she didn't have time to sit down and settle. So, she'd tossed and turned and dreamed of what she was missing until she could bear it no more.

Some of Toni's earliest memories were of listening to her parents whispering together at the campfire while they thought she was sleeping, about all the things they would do when their little girl was older, old enough to be on her own. You could only travel so far when you had a kid who needed things. Her parents loved her, but they had always looked forward to being a couple again too. They had finally gotten that part of their lives back when they died. It had been their third trip alone together, leaving her to run the house while they went to play in the surf and the sand, but they'd never made it home. At least, not alive.

Toni had spent a long time wondering if, in their last moments, they'd wished they'd had more time living the lifestyle they'd both dreamed of for so long. *She* certainly wished they had had the time.

A sharp knocking sound on the window sent Toni scurrying from her warm, comfortable bed to see what crazy thing was happening now. Behind the soft blue curtain, there was a large blue-black bird that looked suspiciously like the large raven that had been perched on the sign above the lady with tarot cards' beautiful house. The rising sun glinted off his glossy feathers, leaving him wreathed in a halo of light. She stared at him for a moment and he stared at her.

After that moment, she reached for the old hand crank and opened the window enough for the bird. Again, it stared at her.

"Mr. Raven, it is really cold outside, and I don't think I want to leave this window open all day. You're welcome to come in. I think I might even be able to drum up a treat for you, but it's got to be one or the other."

The large bird made a low clicking sound and stepped into the room, fluffing and shaking his beautiful dark plumage.

"Aren't you absolutely beautiful?" Toni looked around for something to give the bird.

"Hello," he squawked back to her, watching her as she moved about the room.

"And so smart. I've only ever heard ravens talk in Internet videos before. How awesome are you?" Toni grabbed up a bag of unsalted peanuts she had in her purse. "I really hope you can eat nuts."

Carefully, Toni put a few nuts on the windowsill and watched as the bird looked at the nuts, looked at her, then finally decided they were worthy of further attention. He pecked and moved them, and it looked like he was inspecting them. He made a strange sort of purring cackle sound, plucked up a peanut, made a sort of bow to her, and left the room.

Toni went to the window and called after him. "You're welcome." before shutting the window and cleaning up the rest of the peanuts.

After a quick shower, she dressed in simple black jeans and a black and silver sweater, putting her hair up in an easy twist secured with a thin silver barrette. Her wound barely required a bandage at all now, which still seemed a little strange, for all the pain and the damage there had been. She kept her makeup light with hints of her signature silver. On the way out, she snagged two beautiful fluffy biscuits smeared with blackberry butter, a fruit spread that wasn't quite a jam or jelly and smelled—and tasted—like she imagined manna or ambrosia did. She didn't think she'd ever had cooking as good as Vor's in her life.

She didn't necessarily want to go back to the most beautiful house she'd ever seen, but she wanted to make sure she had the right kind of treats, on the off-chance Mr. Raven ever took to knocking at her chamber window again. She hoped that he would and that he'd let her pet him too.

Mr. Raven sat perched on the sign, chuffing at her as Toni passed by and stepped into the beautiful house. Max appeared nearly immediately again, and Toni didn't even let her say hello. "The raven outside, is he yours?"

"He's an animal. He belongs to no one." The woman was still both the plainest and the most beautiful woman Toni had ever seen, depending on the angle at which Toni looked at her. She found herself shifting to see her from different angles to see if it changed. Max was still wreathed in the smoky gray purple haze. She didn't seem to notice or, if she did, it didn't bother her. The mirror said Toni's aura was still the ugly gray soup it had been before.

Toni rolled her eyes. "Don't be pedantic, you know exactly what I mean."

Max laughed. "He does, sort of. I feed him. I tended to him when he was injured, and he stays close."

"Did you send him to check up on me?"

"What?" Actual confusion crossed the beautiful and plain woman's face before she composed herself again. "I promise you, I've not asked him to do a thing."

Toni absolutely believed her and that made no sense at all. "Does he have a thing for the inn maybe?"

Max shook her head. "I can't remember anyone ever saying anything about him coming to visit anyone before, at the inn or anywhere else. Truly, Ms. Bell. It's interesting though, isn't it?"

"I'm not a fan of interesting so much."

Max laughed a little too brightly. "Are you enjoying your time in Bear Ridge?"

"I don't think I can answer that yet."

"I think you can, but maybe you don't want to. There's a difference." Max sniffed the air for something Toni couldn't smell. "The coffee is ready. Would you like some?"

"Um."

"I do understand, really, and I promise I won't read you, your cards, or your coffee grounds when you're done. I couldn't anyway. I use a regular old coffee pot and that's not the proper way to do readable grounds." She sighed and her shoulders sagged. "I don't generally read people who don't want to be read. Sometimes I can't help it and I'm usually better at keeping things to myself when I need to."

"You absolutely could have helped it. You continued even when I told you I didn't believe." Toni felt a little chuffed that Max wasn't owning her intrusion.

She pressed her lips into a pale line. "I apologize for overstepping. I will do my best to leave you be while you remain in Bear Ridge."

Toni took a deep breath. "A cup of coffee would be great. Thank you."

Max motioned for Toni to follow her back, through the door marked "No Admittance" in elegant silver scroll.

"It startled the heck out of me when he said 'Hello.' I don't think I've ever heard a raven talk before."

Max stopped at the entrance of her kitchen, glancing over her shoulder at Toni. "He spoke to you? He must really think you're something, Ms. Bell. He doesn't speak to most people, only those he sees something special in."

Toni felt a little thrill to know he saw something in her. "Is it okay that I gave him a peanut? Is there something better I can give him?"

"He loves shiny things, from jewelry to bottlecaps, but if you don't have anything you're willing to lose, nuts work fine in a pinch. It speaks volumes that you ask at all." She smiled before allowing Toni into the room.

At once, Toni felt the air change. The kitchen was large and open. A wall of windows looked out into the plant-filled solarium, and a huge stone fireplace with a thick wooden mantel with fat candles, old-looking bottles of herbs and liquids, bowls of salt, and chunks of crystal made the place look exactly what she'd expect the kitchen of an old-school witch to look like. Most of the rest of the kitchen was quite modern and straight out of some glossy magazine. It was the strangest combination and it worked really well for Max. There were bundles of drying herbs and flowers, copper pots, and strings of garlic hanging from an iron filigree over a beautiful granite-topped island, a state-of-the-art gas range, refrigerator, and a bright copper backsplash accenting the dark wood cabinets. Max pulled two thick black mugs from a cabinet and poured the coffee. "Cream or sugar?"

"No, thanks. Black is preferable."

"I admit, I need a smidge of honey in either my tea or coffee." Max stirred her coffee with a delicate spoon. "I'm sorry if I upset you at our first meeting."

"No, you aren't," Toni said.

It looked like Max was about to argue for a moment and then she changed her mind. "You know what? I'm really not. You aren't going to be receptive to the things I want to say to you and I don't know what to do with that. It's a new feeling for me."

"It's new that someone might doubt you?"

"Actually, yes." She handed Toni her coffee. "You really aren't any more receptive today, but I'm not going to be the one who makes you see. I am here to give you the information you should know, regardless of whether or not you believe any of it. Are you willing to sit here for a minute and actually listen to me before you go flouncing off again?"

Toni swallowed her own chuckle. "I didn't flounce exactly."

"You did too."

"Okay, fine. You're right. I did." She smiled and sipped her coffee. It was good but not quite as good as Nana's coffee had been the day before.

"If you really want to make the raven happy, he prefers meat—but not jerky, that's too salty." She opened a cupboard and reached in, pulling out a small waxed bag. "I make him special treats. I'll give you some. I really do appreciate your checking first, and so do all of his internal organs."

"Thanks." Toni tucked the baggy of dried meat strips into her pocket. "You make a lovely cup of coffee."

"But not as good as Nana." Max laughed.

Toni paused and narrowed her eyes at Max. "Did you hear my thoughts?"

"Hell no, I happen to think that on my own." There was no malice in her voice, only mirth. "Anyone who's been to see Nana has trouble with anyone else's coffee. It's a thing that will stay with you when you leave this place, but you won't exactly remember why."

"I don't understand."

"And that's really why you've come to me. For treats too, but you could have asked Syn or Vor for that as easily." Max motioned for Toni to have a seat at the ancient round table. "Bear Ridge isn't like other places. There is magic here, alive in a far more noticeable way than it is in other places. No one knows how old the town is or where it started. We don't think it stays in once place. It might not even really *be* in the same way that other cities are. I know that's confusing."

"It is, but I sort of understand what you mean. It's sort of like a pocket universe, connected but separate, and not all the rules are the same."

"You get it, but you don't yet believe it, right?"

"Pretty much. Would you? In my place, would you believe it?"

"I can't say what I would do in your position. I've always understood magic. You will come to, and if you don't, it won't matter because you will forget it all. When you leave Bear Ridge, your memories of it will cease to be. My understanding from people who've made it back, purely by accident or fate, the general memories of events might be there, but the specifics, names and faces and places, aren't. We've had people live here for most of their lives who leave and remember they had wonderful childhoods but not where or with whom."

"I would think that would be a scary thing for anyone."

Max shrugged. "My understanding from talking to others is that it's a warm feeling of happy and contentment and leaves them with a good impression of their missing time, so they might not think about it much, if at all. I think maybe it's less that they don't remember as much as it is that it never occurs to them to remember. The memories are still there but not accessed."

"So, when I leave here, I won't ever think about it again?" Toni stared at her.

"Correct."

"That's really kind of horrible. I can't imagine forgetting my childhood because I wanted to move somewhere else." Toni finished her coffee.

"You'll find there's more to Bear Ridge than forgetting, and it's for the safety of our people that it happens. We have a lot of people here who would not benefit from being remembered in a real, physical sort of way."

"What? Like they're on the run?"

"No. Not exactly. Though I'm sure they felt like it sometimes. No. I mean it when I say that this place draws magic. Magic in the real sense of the word. All those mythologies, all those religions, they came from somewhere, don't you think? The best stories, the ones that move us, the ones that spur us to be better people, more caring people, they all have a root in truth."

"What exactly are you telling me?" Toni felt her brain stutter, rejecting the notion that half of the words coming out of Max's mouth were anything approaching the truth.

"I'm telling you that some of the people you meet here in Bear Ridge aren't what you think they are. I'm about to have work to do, if you don't mind."

"Oh. Of course." Toni picked up her mug and carried it over to the sink where she gave it a quick wash and set it in the drying rack.

"You didn't have to do that."

"I know. Thank you for the coffee and the story. And the meat." Toni slung her purse over her shoulder.

"Thank you for stopping by and not laughing at me, even if you don't believe in us yet."

Toni wasn't sure if she did or didn't believe the things she was seeing or hearing. She knew Bear Ridge was special and some of the people in it were too. That made Bear Ridge a little dangerous for her own wellbeing. As she pulled open the door, a young couple jumped back. "Oh. I'm sorry. You've got excellent timing though."

The young woman in a puffy green coat smiled brightly at her. "I'm pretty sure it's the other way around. You must be Toni."

She sighed, unsure how to respond.

"I don't mean to be pushy or strange. I promise, he isn't gossiping, but you've made quite the impression on my brother-in-law, Nico."

"Brother-in-law?"

"I'm Nico's brother, Arthur," the man piped up.

"Oh. Dent." The conversation popped back into Toni's head and she smiled, sticking her hand out politely. "It's nice to meet you."

"I'm Melanie." The woman took Toni's hand and clasped it warmly. "I heard you're kind of stuck with us for a bit."

"Until my ride is roadworthy again, yep." She smiled, trying to be polite and still disengage.

"If you aren't busy tonight, it's the beginning of the Winter Festival and the night we do the totem tree. I know you're probably going to be asked by a lot of people today, but, if you'd like, we'd love to have you join our sled."

"Your what?"

"We all get out to the meadow on horse and reindeer-drawn sleighs. We happen to have an extra spot in ours—well three, actually, because Jen's too pregnant to go and Bran would never leave her alone." She shook her head. "Sorry. Too much information. If you want to come, you can. We'll make a stop at the inn at about six. If Nico knew I was asking you, he'd probably pitch a fit. Sorry. You should come. It's fun."

"What's a totem tree?"

Arthur put a hand up and smiled lovingly at his wife. "Come with us. We'll explain it on the way, you'll have a great time, and honestly, you want my other brother, Grey, to tell it. He's the best storyteller of the lot of us."

"Okay." Toni smiled and took a step past them. "It sounds great. Really. But—"

"Nope." Arthur shook his head. "Don't make your mind up now. We'll see you at six and you can decide then."

The couple disappeared into Max's store and Mr. Raven made a noise that sounded suspiciously like laughter.

***

Toni had decided not to go at all until she saw Syn and Vor all dressed up in beautiful long winter dresses, packing up huge baskets of food and jugs of mulled wine, mead, and apple cider. She watched them for a few minutes as they worked in tandem, like a couple who had been together for decades. Vor had her blonde hair in two long braids whereas Syn's was all wound up on top of her head. Syn wore red, Vor wore black, and they both wore aprons embroidered with little animals.

"Is everyone who goes to the festival thing supposed to dress up?" Toni asked. Vor looked up at her and smiled.

"It's certainly not mandatory. Most people do though. It's for fun." Vor shared a meaningful look with Syn. "I have a winter cape you can borrow, and I bet we can figure something out if you don't have something you think will work."

Syn held up a finger as if to shush her. "Don't argue. We haven't had someone to fuss over in years, we'd really like it if you would let us. We don't have a lot of time, certainly not enough to whip up something from scratch but you're an easy size to find. Ten? Eight? Something in there?"

Toni nodded along. It could be interesting to see what they managed to pull together, and she didn't really have anything that was both pretty and warm. And they were going to let her borrow a winter cape. Who could argue with a winter cape? "Please don't go too crazy, okay? Simple."

"No problem. Hair up, makeup clean with a rosy tone. Do you prefer gold or silver?"

"I honestly don't care. I tend to wear both." She held up her right hand where she had her mother's silver wedding band and her father's gold wedding band twinned together into one ring on her middle finger.

"That's lovely." Vor smiled at her with true warmth. "We'll all focus on keeping it simple and elegant. You're so pretty that you don't need a lot of decoration."

"Thanks." Toni blushed a little. "I'll leave it all in your capable hands and go try and get my hair up."

"I should be up in about half an hour, maybe less. Depending." Syn waved her away and Toni did as she was told.

It wasn't terribly long before there was a knock on her door. Toni had managed to fight her hair up into a decent French twist with a few curled tendrils framing her face. She expected Vor or Syn, but it was neither of them at her door. "Can I help you?" Toni pulled the long cardigan currently serving as a robe a little tighter to herself.

"Toni?" The woman standing there wore one of the most exquisite dresses Toni had ever seen in her life. It looked like delicate silver pine sprays artfully laid over a white satin strapless gown with white gloves that covered most of her arms. "I'm Krissy. Vor called my aunt and she asked me to bring this over for you."

Toni took the garment bag gently. "Is this some sort of fancy dance kind of thing?"

"No. The dressing up part is for fun. Most people won't be wearing anything as fancy as my gown or yours for that matter. It's actually a pretty short evening, a beautiful sleigh ride, a bit of a reception with food and conversation, the crowning of the Cardinal Queens, and the totem tree. Then a bit more drinking and another sleigh ride. It's great fun. You'll have a blast."

"Are you a Cardinal Queen?"

Krissy laughed and shook her head. "Not this year. My Aunt Philomena, she basically uses me as a walking advertisement for all the other grand parties during the year. Tonight, you get to be one too. I'd love to stay and get to know you, but I have two more dresses to drop off before heading out to the meadows. You're going to look marvelous. This shade will really offset all those lovely coppery red tones. Hopefully, we can kibbutz at the party."

She swirled away from the door and down the staircase like an old Hollywood starlet, all grace and poise.

Toni closed the door and got her first look at the dress. She'd never worn anything as rich or as fancy in her entire life. Hell, she'd never even touched anything as rich or fancy. Two dainty silver shoes with kitten heels were tucked in the bottom of the bag, wrapped in plastic. Somehow, they'd managed to get the size of her feet right without asking. Maybe Max was right and magic really did live in Bear Ridge.

The dress was something straight off the red carpet, and Kristy was spot-on about the color; it suited her exceptionally well. It was not quite floor-length, made of velvet the color of dark toned emeralds with a scalloped V-neck and cap sleeves. The little silver clutch barely had enough room for her peachy nude lipstick and a bit of cash. It was always better to be prepared.

She descended the staircase—and she had never *descended* anything before, but that was absolutely the right word for it. Vor and Syn were waiting at the bottom, huge smiles on their faces. "You look stunning." Syn kissed her cheek. "Now to keep you warm on the way to the party and back."

Vor flung a fur-lined ash gray cape over Toni's shoulders.

"This is too much. Truly. I feel like Cinderella." When Toni looked in the mirror, she honestly felt like a princess.

"Everyone should get to play Cinderella at least once." Syn grinned.

"Does that make us your fairy godmothers?" Vor giggled like a little girl.

"I should be so lucky." She pulled them both into a hug. "I have no idea what brought me here, but right now, in this moment, I'm so glad it did."

The bells over the door jingled and Nico walked in. He stopped in the doorway and stared, his mouth slightly agape, his dark hair flecked with melting snowflakes. "Wow."

Toni blushed and took in his dark tux and wished he wasn't so damned nice to look at. "Wow, back at you."

"We'll see you there," Vor said. "Enjoy the ride." Vor and Syn linked arms and watched as Toni left with Nico.

Toni nearly tripped over herself, grateful for Nico's steady arm, as she saw the long red sleigh draped with swags of greenery and ribbon. It had seating for six, drawn by two beautiful black horses. Two other couples sat, happy smiles on their faces, tucked into great blankets.

"I'm so glad you decided to come." Melanie waved to her. "You remember Arthur, and this is Daisy and Grey." The other bundled couple waved and said hello in unison.

"Hi." Toni waved awkwardly to the group and tried not to slip on the slick sidewalk.

"I hope you don't mind sitting in front with me," Nico said. "I'm the driver tonight."

"I've never ridden in a sleigh before." She climbed up into the front seat with a little help from Nico and the large block he set down for her. "This is so neat. You do this every year?"

"Yep." He hung the block back on its hook and hoisted himself up into the sleigh, tucking them both in under a thick blanket—maybe a little closer than they strictly needed to be, but Toni wasn't about to complain. "We love Christmas here. Actually, we love all holidays here. Especially the winter ones."

As they rode through the town, other sleighs joined the procession, some jingling, some covered, some open, some pulled by horses, others by what looked like reindeer—and one pulled by a pair of goats. "Are all these people dressed to the nines?"

"No. Honestly, a lot of us think it's fun to dress up, but you'll see people in jeans and sweaters too. No one cares. I was going to wear jeans myself until word came down through the wire, as it does. You look amazing, by the way, since I was too tongue-tied to tell you properly before." He nudged her in a playful way, hands too busy with the reins to hold hers.

"Thanks. You look pretty terrific yourself. Now, what are the Cardinal Queens and what on earth is a totem tree?"

He laughed. "Cardinal Queens are the heads of festivities for the year. They get crowned at the Winter party and we vote at the Halloween party on the next year's queens. They represent the four cardinal directions, each representing a specific season and a specific color. The totem tree is something we decorate. At the end of the night, totems will be handed out and we'll put them on the big tree; it's sort of like getting the fortune from the fortune cookie. Each animal represents your year's prediction. It's a bit of silly fun, and maybe we get a little something to think about for the coming year. We eat, we drink, we laugh, and we get to spend time together. Celebrations in the darkest part of the year remind us that there are good days and good things to come. It's been going on for as long as people have congregated together."

The sleigh slid over the packed snow, the moon making the whole road sparkle like glitter on velvet as they wound their way through the lit-up town and into the woods, the path punctuated by iron light posts adorned with red bows. At the end of the road, several young men in heavy parkas directed the parking. "Would you mind going in with my brothers and their wives? I need to get the horses taken care of really quickly."

"No problem."

Relief passed over Nico's face as he helped her down out of the sleigh and handed the box to his brother, Arthur. "Promise you won't go finding a prince charming while you're waiting on me."

"No problem." Toni stood sort of awkwardly, waiting for Melanie to climb down out of the sleigh. As the women climbed down, Toni finally felt a little less overdressed and out of place. Melanie wore a 1950s-style dress in vibrant red with tiny white snowflakes embroidered on the bodice. The other woman, Grey's wife, Daisy, wore a butter yellow dress and a crown of metal daisies tied into her tiny braids.

"Philomena picked the perfect dress for you, didn't she? It looks really wonderful on you." Melanie tucked Toni's hand in the crook of her arm. "A lot of people will probably come and try and sweep you away. You're pretty well the talk of the town right now, after all."

"There are other tourists in town, aren't there? I can't be the only one." She clenched her teeth in a strange grimace.

"No, you aren't, but you are the prettiest and the most interesting. And you destroyed your car to save a dog. And you've irritated Max twice and aren't trembling in your pretty little shoes. And, to top it all off, you're stuck here, and that never happens. Yeah, everyone is taking a bit of a special interest in you. Am I right in thinking maybe that makes you a little uncomfortable?" Melanie led her into a huge barn with fairy lights draped with greenery on the walls, and huge old-style candle chandeliers hung from thick wooden rafters. Food and drinks covered several tables along one wall, other empty tables sat waiting for people to sit at them, and big fat candles surrounded by greenery and ribbon sat in the centers. An enormous, quite empty tree filled one corner.

Toni felt every pair of eyes in the building turn to her, and it was an awful lot of pairs of curious eyes. "A lot uncomfortable, actually. I'm used to being the center of attention; I get on stage on purpose, but that's different than this. This feels intrusive and weird. You all know a lot more about me than I know about any of you."

"I don't think that's true of all of us, though. I think there's two or three you're getting to know well." Melanie waved to Syn and Vor who were emptying their baskets onto the snack tables. "I know they think you're the bee's knees."

"They're sweet."

"They are." Melanie nodded. "I don't want to be the protective bitchy one, but I am. These are my friends, this is my home. I don't want to see my friends get hurt. Especially my dorky brother-in-law."

"I appreciate your stance. I find it refreshing. I promise, I've made it abundantly clear that I'm getting back on the road as soon as my truck is put back together. I'm not here to mess anyone up or hurt anyone. You get travelers through here all the time. I'm no different than any of them."

Melanie stopped walking and looked at Toni, really inspecting her face. "The funny thing is, Toni, I think you actually believe that. I'll leave you to your date now, though. Have fun tonight."

Toni didn't get a chance to respond—even if she'd known how to—before Nico was standing next to her, smelling even better than he looked. It was flat criminal how perfect he was. She didn't pull away when he took her hand in his or when he led her around the great hall, stopping occasionally to introduce her to someone or say hello to someone else. As they walked, they sampled the foods: a spiced fruit bread called barm brack, a Christmas pudding, some prosciutto skewers with melon and a mellow white cheese, all sorts of cookies and cakes, and some sort of pancake kind of thing called svele. Nico handed her a bottle of Christmas soda called Julmust that was interesting but didn't quite leave a lasting impression on her.

About an hour into what really was only a party and not any sort of dance, the mayor, Trevor Gibson, appeared with a microphone and started talking. It took a minute for everyone to settle and quite down. Cardinal Queens were representatives of the seasons. Toni couldn't help the smile that bloomed as Syn and Vor came to the center of the room with Max and another woman. Syn in red for summer, Vor in black for winter, Max in steely blue for autumn, and the fourth woman named Stacy in yellow for spring. Apparently, they were responsible for all of the community festivities and parties for the year and the new Cardinal Queens would be responsible for the next year's festivities. Starting with Nana from Teas Me as the new winter, Philomena, the woman who sent the dress, as the new autumn, a woman named Ashley as the new summer, and Jo from the diner as the new spring, the former queens passed along their embroidered aprons with hugs and smiles and the ceremony was finished.

It seemed to Toni like a pretty lavish party for announcing the following year's party planners.

"They're going to be bringing a table around," Nico whispered in her ear. "Take whatever little white box feels like the right one for you."

"It's not that loud in here, you don't need to whisper." Toni leaned slightly away so she could see him better.

"But if I whisper, I get to be close enough to smell your soap. What is it? Honeysuckle?"

"Yes, actually. You've got a good nose. I'm supposed to pick a box? How do I know which one to pick?" she asked.

"Be the Roman for a minute, Toni." Nico said with a sly smile.

She sighed and watched as the cart moved through the room, stopping at each person. The pile of little white boxes got smaller as it went but it still seemed to have more boxes. They were each about three inches cubed, tied with twine. The boxes looked old, like they'd been used for this event for decades and might fall apart at any moment. She did as she was instructed, plucking a box for herself as the cart went by. She looked around, watching as people opened their boxes, each pulling out a small animal ornament that they took and hung on the enormous tree in the corner.

"Well? What'd you get?" Nico made the little brown dog in his hand dance.

Toni untied the twine, lifted the lid, and nearly groaned as she pulled the delicate glass raven from the bed of cotton fluff it laid on. "What's it mean?"

"There's a little slip of paper inside the box also. You should read it." He grinned.

The paper taped inside the lid of the box had a few simple lines of text. "It will be a fortuitous and transformative year. The universe is telling you all you need to know. Listen." She was quiet for a beat before changing the subject. "What's your dog mean?"

"It means I'm a stable sort of man, loyal, loveable, open. And that this year is going to be worth the effort." He smiled at her and stepped aside as Vor and Syn approached. "You guys did a great job this year. The new Cardinals have a lot to live up to."

Vor shook her head with a shy smile. "Are you enjoying yourself?"

"Very much," Toni said with more genuine pleasure than she'd meant to admit. "The town does stuff like this often?"

"One or two times a season, yes. We're a small community and it gets boring here sometimes. It keeps us from going bonkers." Syn held up her little totem, an eagle. "It's time to decorate the tree. Come on."

"What's your fortune mean?"

"Well, I got an eagle which means that this year is all about hope and balance. Vor got a bear, so, for her, it's all about enjoying the simple pleasures in life and nurturing her family. And now, we need to put them up on the tree."

"Is this a sort of tradition that comes from somewhere or something?"

"No." Syn answered. "I think this is entirely a Bear Ridge and a Max thing. We've been doing it for a long time, almost as long as I can remember, in various ways. I think it started with painted stones as gifts left on porches as good omens for the year to come. For me, it's been more or less true year after year. I find myself noticing my given animal more, seeing it more, hearing about it more, and generally seeing more of its traits in myself. Maybe it makes us a little more reflective and intuitive."

"Like any and all fortune sorts of thing." Toni joined the line that formed as people headed to the tree to hang their fortunes. "Why the tree though?"

"I suppose it is so they don't have to get new totems every year," Syn said.

"I think it's because it lends a feeling of community, for all of us to come together to decorate this big beautiful tree together, each of us looking toward the next year with hope and promise." Vor sounded a bit wistful and maybe even a little sad. "I always found this to be quite a lovely tradition."

***

The evening wound down after the tree trimming. People went back for treats they'd missed and were handed boxes to take home with them. Plans were made for the coming days among friends. Toni watched with more interest than longing and never once felt out of place or unwanted. Everyone and their brother make a point to say hello to Toni before they headed back out into the cold night to load up the sleighs and the horses and go home again.

When Nico dropped her off in front of the Bear Ridge Inn, Toni didn't back away from his kiss. Too many thoughts circled her mind, but they all went silent when Nico's lips touched hers. She leaned in to his touch without even realizing it. It would be so easy to give in and let go. Instead, she pulled back. "I had a lovely night. Thank you."

"Thank you for coming." He went to kiss her again, and Toni took a step back, putting distance between them.

"You have other passengers to see home yet, so good night, Nico." She let herself into the inn and did not look back, however badly she wanted to.

Chapter Four

When Toni woke, she wasn't the least bit surprised to find that the clock read nearly eleven. She'd had a much better time the night before than she'd expected. Bear Ridge was a little bit odd but a lot interesting. She imagined anthropologists could have a blast writing about the town and their crazy claims and rather folksy traditions.

Before she'd even pulled herself out of bed, the tapping started on her window. She groaned and got up and cranked the window open. "Good morning, Mr. Raven. I'm not quite awake yet, but please, do come in and keep me company while I get myself halfway put together."

The bird hopped into the room and looked at her, quietly clicking away.

"I had a wonderful time last night, thanks for asking." She dug out the little baggie of meat and pulled a strip out for him. "As a matter of fact, I got you for the totem tree. How did you manage that?"

Toni tried not to but couldn't help flinching as the raven snapped the meat from her fingers. "You'll have to be gentle with me, I've never fed any bird before. Can I pet you?"

The bird looked at her as if he understood and cocked his head to the side, offering a place for her to scratch on his neck. It was more than a little thrilling to be feeding him, let alone petting him. He seemed to understand what she was saying and to know a great deal—not that he could tell her in so many words. She'd probably never have another experience like this when she left Bear Ridge, so she intended to get as much out of it as she could while she could.

When he was done being touched, the large bird hopped back to the window and was gone again. It was the closest she'd ever been to a wild animal, or any bird for that matter. Having company was nice.

She thought about what it would take to get a dog to travel with her after she left Bear Ridge. She hadn't been allowed as a kid, but there was no one to tell her no now. If she wanted to adopt a dog and lug him from beach to beach or town to town, that was on her head. It wasn't like she couldn't find places where dogs were allowed and there were a lot of dogs out there who needed homes. And then she wouldn't be alone all the time.

Toni washed and dressed, throwing on work clothes and rounding up all the rest of her clothes for laundering. She'd have to find a laundromat while she was out returning the dress. Except that the dress, shoes, and the bag they came in were not where she'd put them. More than a little confused, she rushed down the steps and nearly plowed into Syn. "Did you by chance take that dress out of my room?"

"Dress?" She looked at Toni for a second before realization washed over her. "Oh, yes. I was headed over that direction this morning to discuss a few things with Philomena and hand over the keys to the Cardinal Queen offices, so I figured I'd save you the trip. I'm sorry. Sometimes I don't think before I do things."

"Oh, no, that's okay. I was a little worried."

"It's funny but I'd never think to do that for another resident here, so I must apologize sincerely for overstepping. I don't even understand why I did it." Syn looked quite confused.

"I appreciate that you see that. It really isn't that big a deal. At least not right now." Toni smiled and decided a little truth wouldn't hurt her to give away. "I sort of understand. It feels a little like I've known you and Vor for a lot longer than I have, and it's really easy to slip and slide into that familiar place when you've been so kind as to let me work off some of my bill and still stay in probably the most beautiful place I've ever stayed in my life."

"You're helping us as much as we're helping you." Syn smiled and looked a little less apologetic.

"Is there a laundromat in town?"

"Yes, but if you don't mind doing a few loads of bedding along with it, you can use the machines in the basement." Syn pulled a key ring out of her pocket and handed it to her. "The door is marked Employees Only and next to the powder room in the hall. There's detergents, softeners, additives, nearly anything you might need."

"Thanks. Is the bedding down there or do I need to collect it?"

"In the laundry room there will be a pile right under the laundry chute. I certainly don't expect you to do all of it. We run loads a few times a day when we're not too terribly busy. I don't think we've ever—even temporarily—conquered that mountain, but every now and again we see the summit." Syn lowered her voice and leaned in close. "Sometimes, we say screw it and get new linens for everyone."

Toni laughed, as she was meant to. "Well, I've got nothing better to do today than see how far I can get."

"Good luck."

"It sounds like I'm going to need it." Toni took the key and headed for the basement. She'd start up a load of sheets and then put together her own laundry. It had only been a few days, but more and more, the Bear Ridge Inn felt like home and it certainly wasn't about the house. The pile of laundry was bigger than Toni had envisioned. For a town full of magic, it needed little laundry fairies or the elves that visited the cobbler in that old children's story. Of course, with her luck, she'd be more likely to get a Rumpelstiltskin instead, and nobody needed that.

It only took her a few minutes to get two loads going. Her benefactors obviously hated doing laundry, given how much they let it back up despite the fact that they had two sets of washers and dryers. She looked around the room and found an ironing board, a serviceable iron probably from the 1970s, and a drying rack. Everything she needed to get it done.

Toni didn't mind doing laundry. It felt productive and a lot like self-care. While the first sets of sheets were getting agitated, Toni used the deep sink and some elbow grease to wash up her underwear and bras and put them on the rack. It was nice not having to hang them over the curtain rod in a bathroom or on a line strung from her truck to a tree.

By the time her two loads of laundry hit the dryers, she was pretty well out of things to do except watch fabric dry. The basement was oddly set up. At the bottom of the steps was a clean but out-of-date lounge room that stank slightly of faded old cigar smoke. It wasn't much, only a sitting room with two metal and vinyl chairs and an ancient threadbare wingback lounger with a small coffee table that held a few magazines that were nearly a decade old. The laundry room, a small powder room, and a workroom split off from it. The laundry room was brightly painted and clean, but chock-full of laundry, a chore Toni decided to claim until her truck was done, given how much there was to do. The workroom looked like it had once seen a great deal of use but there was a solid layer of dust on most of the tools now. A few screwdrivers and a hammer were the only things that looked like they'd even been acknowledged in at least five years.

Curiosity and not a little boredom had Toni peeking into the vast storage rooms under the inn. Most things were in boxes, but she could see a few things in the dim light of the single exposed bulb. It looked like her ladies had once been cosplayers or actors. The ancient looking armor she could see looked far too detailed and intricate for a costume; it was definitely prop level. Her stomach rumbled a bit and she remembered that she'd forgotten to eat breakfast.

As she was putting together a quick sandwich from the breakfast feast's leftovers, Syn came into the kitchen with a tray of cups from the various rooms. "How goes the mountain?"

"I'm making a dent. I've got two loads of sheets all the way done and two in the washers. Mine should be dry enough to iron as soon as I'm done eating."

"Wow. That's a lot of headway in so short a time."

"You were kind enough to take care of the only chore I had for myself today so it's not like I don't have time to help. You want a sandwich?"

"Oh, no thanks. I ate a little while ago with Vor."

"So, which one of you is the actor?"

Syn looked at her strangely. "What?"

"I was being nosy, and you've got some beautiful prop armor down there. I figure either stage or convention. I can't imagine conventions being a thing that comes through here, though."

"No, I can't say I've ever been to a convention." She shook her head. "I honestly don't think you'd believe me if I told you what that is."

"You're not going to tell me something crazy, are you?"

"I think, if I told you the truth, you would think it's completely crazy." She smiled but there was sadness in her voice too.

"Look, we're already probably a little more familiar than I expected us to be," Toni said. "I don't get close to people. I don't, I can't. And yet, here we are anyway. I adore you both. I can't promise I'll necessarily believe you; there's a big part of me that feels like I've got to be on some hidden camera show. I don't think I'll think less of you either."

Syn pursed her lips tight together. "Give me a second. This one isn't only mine to tell. Don't go anywhere."

"I've no intention of going anywhere right now." Toni watched as Syn hurried out of the room, ostensibly to find Vor. She knew it was going to be something crazy. They were going to tell her something that would be really hard to believe, and she was going to have to figure out what she thought about *all* of Bear Ridge, not only her temporary housemates.

As she swallowed the last bite of her sandwich, the bells over the door jingled and a panicked male voice started calling for Syn. Toni rushed to the entry and arrived behind Syn and Vor. The man in the entry was wringing his hands but grinning, his smile unmistakable.

"Is it time?" Syn asked calmly.

"It is. It is. Her mom's already taken her over to Doctor Cait and she wanted me to get you. I know she wanted me to get you for the sake of having something productive to do for a minute so I can focus on something that's not her or the baby, or my own freaking out. I know I'm totally freaking out." His words came too fast. His excitement nearly had him vibrating.

Vor turned to Toni. "His wife is about to have their first child. Bran is sort of an excitable sort."

"I gathered." Toni watched him closely as something seemed a little off, a little blurry, like she couldn't actually see him clearly.

"I'll get my bag and meet you there. By the time you get over to the health center, she should be all checked in. You let her know that I'm on my way." Syn ushered him back out the door. "Everything is going to be okay. Take a deep breath and think good thoughts. You guys are ready for this."

"I know. Thanks. She'll feel better once you're there. I will too." He hugged Syn and headed back to his waiting and running car.

"Syn is Bear Ridge's best midwife." Vor beamed with pride.

"I'm Bear Ridge's only midwife, love," Syn protested but blushed along with her words. "I'm not sure when I'll be back."

"I know. I'll bring food by if it goes too terribly long." Vor turned to Toni. "Syn told me that you asked about the armor. It looks like our conversation is going to have a wait a few days."

"Of course." Toni nodded. "It must be exciting helping usher in babies."

"It's more fulfilling than exciting. In childbirth, generally speaking, exciting is bad." Syn went to the closet under the grand staircase and pulled out a small leather suitcase. "We're after a nice, calm, if a bit screamy, process."

"Screamy?" Toni cringed thinking about the pain she'd heard about.

Syn laughed as she pulled on her long blue coat. "Some moms are quite loud. I'm pretty sure there's nothing I haven't seen or heard during the process after all these years. I'll be home when I can." Syn kissed Vor goodbye and headed out the door.

"Have you ever given any thought to children?" Vor stared out the window, watching Syn's coat flutter out behind her.

"Thought? Maybe. I don't think they're really in my future though."

"Can I ask why?" Her voice was testing and prodding but not pushy.

Toni appreciated her asking permission that way, but it still felt intrusive and weird. "I'm not really the settling down type. I have too much I haven't done yet to even think about that part of my future."

She made a sort of humming, thoughtful sound. "Either way. I'm going to go get to work on a picnic for the new family for later and a few freezer casseroles for them. If you need anything at all, I'll be in the kitchen."

"No problem. It's about time to flip the laundry around again. Where should I put the laundered linens and towels?"

"There's a big closet in the laundry room. It's not well organized, but that's where we keep everything."

"Gotcha." Toni had seen the closet and figured it was extra stuff rather than what they used all the time. Organized they were not. Years of living in ridiculously small spaces had made organization her forte.

She was happy to have the chores, because she really didn't want to go out at all. She needed to take a giant step back from everyone until her truck was finished. It was already going to be hard enough to leave. And she was *absolutely* leaving. She had places to be, things to see.

While things were washing and drying and airing out, Toni set to work organizing the linen storage. Everything neat, tidy, and in its place. Except for the fitted sheets. Those were not quite tidy or neat, but not a ball of frustrating, maddening fabric either, so Toni counted it as a win. By the time she had her laundry finished, ironed, and put away, the closet at least half finished, and the mountain whittled down to a hill, it was time for dinner. Rather than be a pest, she threw on her freshly washed jeans and a sweater and headed for the diner, crossing her fingers for no Nico.

She was joined on her walk by her vigilant friend as Mr. Raven flew from tree to tree to rooftop to lamppost, following along. In a weird way, it was sweet. It was a much farther walk to the diner than she'd thought it would be, but her coat was warm enough. The town was as pretty and quaint on foot as it had been from the passenger seat of Nico's Jeep, though it had certainly been warmer in the Jeep. She'd be doubly glad when her truck was finished. Winter was a terrible time to be without transportation.

When she reached the diner she was both frozen and starving. Fortunately, the diner was exactly the place to fix both of those problems.

"Evening, Toni." Jo waved to her from behind the counter. "Have a seat wherever and I'll be right with you."

Toni glanced around. It wasn't crowded or too busy, but she didn't want to take up a whole table for one person, so she plunked herself down at the counter instead. "How's it going, Jo?"

"Pretty good. My shift's almost over. It's ladies' night at the Fighting Unicorn, and Kevin's working late, probably on your truck, so I don't feel bad going out with the girls. It's going to be lovely." She was smiling brightly and the bounce in her step was absolutely literal. "Oh. Tell me you don't have plans tonight."

Put on the spot a little, she really didn't know what to say. "Not exactly."

"Wonderful. You'll come with me." She plopped a menu down in front of Toni. "The salmon is really great tonight."

"That sounds fine." Toni nodded. "With water and coffee please."

"You bet." She scribbled words down on her notepad and clipped the sheet up on a metal wheel behind her. She turned back to Toni with a coffee pot in her hand. "I was being serious, in case you didn't know. Come with me to the Unicorn. I promise, you'll have a great time."

"I appreciate the offer, Jo but—"

"Nope. No buts." She walked away with a bounce in her step and Toni shook her head. She hadn't planned to do anything except eat and head back to the inn.

She ate in relative peace as Jo was busy keeping on top of coffee cups and menus until her relief arrived. On the heels of Fred, Jo's relief, a trio of young women near enough to Toni's own age entered the diner and gathered at the counter. Though she hadn't said more than hello and goodbye to her, Toni recognized Daisy, Nico's brother Grey's wife, from the party the night before. The other two she hadn't met.

Jo waved them over to where she was standing with Toni. "Do you ladies mind if Toni comes with? She's passing through and definitely needs to see the Fighting Unicorn before she gets the hell out of Dodge."

The women laughed and Toni realized she'd missed something, some sort of inside joke between the friends. None of them voiced any opposition, and though Daisy didn't seem super thrilled, she wasn't opposed. Jo introduced her to the other two: Wohpe, a beautiful woman in white who looked only a smidge older than Toni, if you didn't look in her eyes, and Seo-yun, a woman of almost thirty who'd once been "passing through" about seven years before. Then Toni understood the joke fine. Seo-yun had been nearly as vehement as Toni was about it being a short visit in Bear Ridge and nothing more. Enough that, seven years later, Seo-yun still talked about moving on but never actually did. And didn't sound like she really wanted to go anywhere either.

Toni paid her bill and gave in, falling in as the fifth member of the party. Jo linked her arm in Toni's and made sure she didn't fall behind. Toni wasn't exactly sure what to do with that, but figured it was one of those times where it was better to give up and go along with it.

The Fighting Unicorn looked like a bar in the wrong country. It looked like Toni thought a good old Irish pub should look. The windows were each set with four panes around a stained-glass circle depicting a small unicorn head. The wood was dark and shone with polish, and the bar was curved slightly before the huge length of mirror with two shelves at the top, full of liquor bottles of all shapes and sizes. The scarred tables were placed at even intervals along the leather bench that ran nearly the whole length of the wall opposite a line of chairs.

"Ladies." The not quite giant of a man behind the bar had a voice to match his body and a smile whiter than snow and truer than north. "I see you've brought me a new young maiden."

Toni's eyebrows shot up in annoyance.

"No." The man shook his head quickly after noticing her expression. "I apologize. I don't know you, and you don't know me. I promise I'm not actually that sort of man. I am many things, and not all of them are necessarily good, however, women are my favorite people and I hold them in the highest esteem. I am an oaf, but not a boorish one."

Toni bit her lip to keep from smiling at his melodramatic bow and apology. Instead, she offered him a small, curt, uppity smile full of sharp edges and a belly laugh.

He clutched at his chest dramatically. "You wound me so. Welcome to the Fighting Unicorn. I am Lou, and the quiet, swarthy one down there is Hue. You are not from around here."

Jo wrapped her arm around Toni's shoulder. "This is Toni. She'll be with us this evening."

A look passed between Daisy and Lou that Toni didn't understand but figured she'd ignore as Jo led her over to the table the girls had claimed. Daisy got the first round while everyone else got situated.

"Lou doesn't mean anything by it. He's a bit of a joker." Daisy sat down next to Toni. "I'm sorry we didn't get a chance to talk much at the party."

"It's a little hard to talk on a sleigh." Toni smiled.

"And Nico has tried to keep you to himself."

Toni sighed. "He's really an amazingly sweet and thoughtful man. He's going to make some girl happy someday."

The women around the table all giggled.

"What?"

"His mom has plans for that." Daisy took a long drink of her beer. "She means well and, as one of her daughters in law, I really do like her, but she's a little excitable and overbearing. With Nico especially. He's sort of her favorite—but please don't tell my husband that."

"I would never."

"She thinks he should marry one of her friend's daughters who is one of his best friends, never mind that she is most assuredly not interested in Nico that way, nor is he interested in her."

"Plus, *she's* got eyes on someone else, thank you very much." Wohpe picked up her drink and nodded at the quiet man at the end of the bar, who Lou had introduced as Hue. "My mother doesn't have to understand why. His mom either, for that matter."

"Oh, you're the 'her.'" Toni put the pieces together. "So, you're probably wanting to warn me to behave like everyone else."

"Nope." Wohpe smiled at her, her black eyes shining. "I think a little bit of fun is exactly what he needs. He's always been a little too future-thinking for my taste. He's a planner. He honestly can't help it. You've told him, and everyone else, that you are here only until your truck gets fixed. He knows that. It isn't your fault if he doesn't listen."

Toni almost wanted to yell at the woman for that. Shouldn't she want to protect Nico from getting hurt from a girl there was zero chance of a future? Isn't that what best friends did? Toni kept her mouth shut though and took a sip of her beer. which was purportedly a Murphy's Irish Stout. She wasn't exactly sure she loved it, but she liked it better than most stouts.

She listened to the girls chatter about people they knew, things going on, and events coming up in town over the next few weeks. She should have felt separate, like an outsider, but she didn't. It almost felt like she'd known these four women for years and not minutes. She understood nearly immediately why Nico and Wohpe were besties—they were pretty much the same person. Happy, friendly, open, smart, and quick-witted while being absurdly calming and comforting. Daisy was definitely the crazy hippie of the bunch, all peace and love and flower power, but she had a little edge to her, if you were watching. The kind of edge that said she knew people who knew how to put the hurt on, should she need them to. Jo was their Maryanne. Sweet, wholesome, and adorable. Seo-yun was quiet and bookish and the most businesslike of them, which made sense as she was a tax attorney. Toni slid a little too easily into their group, as it was lacking in the loud and creative department, and she fit that bill nearly perfectly.

Hue and Lou were excellent bartenders. She watched as they made sure their patrons were happy but not sloppy, and there wasn't even a hint of animosity in the place. They had a stage for live music, darts (which Toni discovered she was passable at), and pool (which she most certainly wasn't). It was the best kind of neighborhood pub. No muss, no fuss, simply a lot of fun with an alcoholic cherry on top.

After they'd been there a few hours, Nico, Grey, and Kevin showed up and sat at the table next to them, settling in before getting up to play pool. They didn't interfere with ladies' night, but the air definitely changed for Jo and Daisy when their husbands arrived. It wasn't a bad change, more like an addition, but Toni found herself staying a little quieter, a little more separate.

When it was her turn to get the round, she headed up to the bar with the tray the others had used and waited patiently for her turn.

Lou smiled broadly at her, his cheeks pinking up a little. "Sorry about earlier. I tend to forget that some people aren't used to me."

"I've seen much worse than you, and you apologized faster than I've ever seen a man do in my life." She smiled, trying to reassure him.

He laughed. "Well then, what can I get for you?" His accent was vaguely Scottish.

"Something a little dark, something a little sweet. Do you have anything that might fit that bill?"

"Hmmm. I think I might. Do you trust me?"

"Not a tiny bit." She smiled.

"Oh, a smart one. I like you." His laugh was loud and infectious. "I think a black and black might be exactly what you need. Guinness, like a good girl, with a touch of black currant. A little dark, a little sweet."

"That sounds about perfect. Do the other girls like that sort of thing? I don't want to screw up my turn."

Lou dropped the act for a minute, his green eyes shining in the dim light of the bar. "It's a good sort that gives a damn about doing right by the people you met. I've never known any of those girls to turn one of these down. I don't know that Seo-yun has ever had one, but she likes Guinness fine and I've never heard tell of any fruit allergies from any of them."

"Then that's what I'd like to do." She dug money out of her purse and added a good tip in the overflowing brandy snifter on the bar.

Lou gave her wink and made up her drinks, putting them on the tray and carrying them to the table. The girls all seemed to like her pick and Toni felt a bit more at ease, having gotten it right. The night ticked on, the crowd got a little bigger, and the musicians that had been busking near the Greek restaurant showed up to do a set. There was a little dancing and Toni thought for sure that Nico would ask her, but she found him twirling Wohpe around the floor instead. She wasn't pleased with the strange pang of jealousy. She was not that sort of girl and she held no claim on him. It was stupid and silly... and yet, she still felt it. She missed his attention more than a little, and that was not what she wanted.

"You look a little lonely." Hue appeared at her elbow, staring at Nico and Wohpe too.

"Lonely is probably not the word I would use." She smiled up at him and then understood what he meant. "Oh. Would you like to dance?"

"I thought you'd never ask." He took her hand in his and spun her around. His palm was warm but the rest of him was a little cool to the touch. His accent was vaguely Brazilian or Portuguese, Toni couldn't tell, and he looked like he stepped off of a runway in Milan. He was beautiful, but his eyes told the truth—he was a devious sort.

They spun around the floor, weaving through couples and groups, slowly and deftly finding themselves next to Nico and Wohpe. Toni didn't see it coming as Hue switched up the partners, putting her with Nico and taking Wohpe for himself. The couple spun away before anyone could protest, but Wohpe's laugh filled the bar.

Toni laughed along with her until she looked into Nico's eyes. He had everything to offer, she had everything to lose, but she looked at him and nothing else mattered. She swayed in his arms and couldn't even hear the music anymore. When he led her back to her drink and her friends, she almost asked him to stay. Almost.

Rather than obsess or even think about it, Toni talked with her new friends and enjoyed the music. She ignored the thrill at the edge of her mind whenever Nico would look over at her. It was juvenile and obnoxious, and she found herself enjoying every minute, staring at him until he looked up and looking away as fast as she could with him doing the same. It felt like high school, fun and flirty in an innocent way, even though there was nothing innocent about how she felt for him.

"Thanks for inviting me out." Toni spoke loud enough to be heard in Jo's ear during one raucous song as they bounced along on the dance floor.

"I'm so glad you said yes."

"Not that you gave me too much of an option."

Jo smiled, her eyes a little glassy from the alcohol. "If I had, you'd have said no."

"You're not wrong." Toni laughed. "I'm gonna head back to the inn now, though. I'm definitely needing some sleep."

"Come by the diner in a few days and we'll do this again."

Toni said her goodbyes to Daisy, Seo-yun, and Wohpe before bundling up and heading out into the night. She wasn't the least bit surprised to find Mr. Raven waiting on the lamppost. "I hope you know where I'm going, Mr. Raven."

The bird ruffled his feathers and looked to her left as if to say, "That way, you ninny."

"Thank you kindly, my favorite bird." Toni bowed slightly and headed in that direction, humming the melody to the song that they'd been playing as she left. She was definitely feeling the alcohol and was glad she hadn't driven.

As if by magic, a Jeep slowed on the road beside her. "It's a long walk back to the inn, Toni."

"Nico/" She smiled at him but didn't move. "What are you doing? You should stay with your friends."

"I'll come back for them. I'm Daisy and Grey's ride home tonight anyway."

"Are you sober?"

"I didn't drink tonight. We take turns. Tonight was Kevin's and my turn to play cab driver. If you're ready to head for the inn, I'm happy to do my job and take you." He shook his head and laughed.

Between the alcohol and her own terribly delicious thoughts, Toni flushed at the idea of being alone with him. "Are you sure?"

"Nothing I'd rather do tonight, m'lady." He hopped out of the Jeep and then helped her up into the passenger seat. "You are a bit more drunk than I thought."

"No. I'm warm and happy, but totally not drunk." She grinned and felt the world sway.

"Whatever you say." He headed toward the inn and she allowed herself to sneak some not-so-subtle glances at him.

"Did you have fun?" he asked.

"I did. More than I have in a long time." Which she hadn't meant to say out loud.

"I'm glad. You made quite the impression on Lou, I heard."

"More he made the impression and I reacted badly. I think it all ended up okay." She stared out the window, watching the town pass by. "You have a beautiful little town here, Nico. I can see why you all love it so much to do all the crazy things."

"Crazy things?"

"Big parties, decorations, crazy people who want me to believe I'll forget all of this when it's done."

"Ah. Unfortunately, that part is really true." And it broke his heart to think about it.

"I won't. I won't forget this place or you. It's all too fantastic to forget."

"If you leave—" his voice got quiet as he pulled to a stop in front of the inn. "When you leave, you'll forget me, Bear Ridge, and everything and everyone here."

Toni laid a hand on his cheek and stared into his eyes, drunk enough to speak and say more than what she wanted to but not drunk enough to let it go further. "You are far too perfect to ever forget." She pressed her lips to his and did her best to ignore the spark that lit in her belly. "Thank you for the ride."

"I really wish I didn't have other people to drive home tonight." Nico stared into her eyes for a moment before getting out of the Jeep and opening her door. He said nothing as she got out but waited until she was safely standing in the open door before getting back in the Jeep and driving off. Toni waved to Mr. Raven who was perched across the street and headed directly for bed.

Chapter Five

Toni woke to the sound of a child crying and her first instinct was to find her and figure out how to help. When she opened her eyes, she realized why the child was in tears. The power was completely out and everything was pitch dark. She thought for a moment about the room and where her purse was. She always had a little pen light in her purse. Using her otherwise useless phone as a light, she located her purse and the little flashlight, pulled on her bathrobe, and headed for the commotion.

Toni knocked on the door at the other end of the hall.

"Come in." A stressed voice on the other side of the door called, and Toni opened the door with her phone in one hand and the little light in the other.

"I thought you might need a little light." She smiled at the crying girl. "May I?"

The girl's mother motioned Toni into the room, disheveled and tired looking. "You must be an angel."

"Nope, I'm a girl who doesn't like the dark either." Toni knelt down in front of the child, who looked to be about nine or ten, who had a short bob of dark hair and huge dark eyes filled with tears. "My name is Toni."

The little girl sniffled and wiped her eyes as she reached for the little pen light Toni was offering.

"I think I saw some hurricane lamps downstairs. If you give me a minute, I can get a couple of them for you and then it won't be so dark and scary anymore."

"Thank you so much." The girl's mother smiled, exhaustion dancing in her eyes.

"I'll be right back." Toni left the little pen light and used her phone's flashlight to get down the stairs and into the dining room.

She remembered seeing the lamps when she was dusting the sideboard. Fortunately, the four she found all had oil in them. She took the smallest of them and lit it, shoving her phone back in the pocket of her robe. She put all of the lights on a silver serving tray and made her way back up the stairs. She knocked lightly on the first door that, if she wasn't mistaken, housed the family with the boys. The father gratefully took one of the large lamps and lit it.

Toni delivered the rest of the lamps to the girl with a smile. "There now, it's not dark anymore."

"Thank you." Her tiny voice still hitched but she was no longer actively crying. She rocked subtly back and forth as she pulled at her fingers.

Toni spotted the little white machine in the corner and barely contained her understanding groan. "You have a hard time when it's super quiet, don't you?" The little girl nodded. "Ma'am?" Toni called to the mother. "I think I can help, if you don't mind."

"Oh, honey, I will never turn down help at one in the morning." She smiled but it didn't quite reach her eyes.

Toni motioned with her head for the mom to follow her for a moment. Once they were out in the hallway, Toni held the lit lamp in her hand. "Um, I don't want to be nosy or anything, but is she on the spectrum?"

"Yes." There was a tentativeness in her voice, as if she was waiting to be judged. Her eyes grew wary and steely at the same time.

"Would music help? I can play for a little while if you want. Maybe we'll luck out and the power will come back soon so you can get her noise machine going."

"You would do that?" Tears glistened in her eyes. Her whole body relaxed, knowing that Toni meant to help.

"Of course. I'll be right back." Toni hurried back to her room and grabbed her guitar. She'd been all over North America and, in her experience, no one appreciated help more than the parents of kids who were a little different. Mostly because they were so used to being judged or admonished for not being strict enough, being too strict, giving in too much, or not giving in enough.

The mother stood at the door near tears herself as she watched Toni actually come back to the room. "You can't know how much this means to me."

Toni shrugged and held out her hand. "I'm Toni."

"I'm Denita, my husband is Chris, and our little girl is Annette."

"Disney fan?"

The woman laughed. "Isn't everybody? Seriously though, she's named for my late grandmother."

Toni stepped closer to the girl, bending low and keeping herself a little small and unintimidating. "Hi, Annette. Do you remember when I told you my name? Everyone calls me Toni, but my name is really Antoinette, and that sounds a lot like Annette, doesn't it?" The girl smiled and started to look a little more comfortable. At least her lips were no longer frozen in a painfully stressed grimace. "Your mom said I can play for you for a little while and maybe it won't be so quiet. Would you like that?"

The little girl nodded vigorously, staring at the beautiful thrift store guitar in Toni's hands.

"Do you have a favorite song, Annette?" Toni tried to remember all of the things she'd been told by other families, not sitting too close or too far, getting down on the floor, on her level, making sure to speak clearly and simply and not to actually expect a response.

"She's really into Christmas carols right now." Her dad, Chris, offered with a smile. He was a wiry man with graying brown hair and kind eyes.

Toni was careful to keep her face blank, with a practiced pleasant smile. It was that time of year with a tiny child. Of course, she would be mostly listening to Christmas music. "I think I know a few of those." She started with a quiet rendition of "Silver Bells," then "White Christmas," and on through the list of all the songs she could remember. By the time she got to "Silent Night," nearly everyone in the inn was standing in the room and in the hallway listening to her play and sing. She spotted Vor in the back watching her with tears of joy in her eyes.

"If you're all going to listen, you should all join in." She picked up the pace a little and picked something a little brighter with a little more pep and started to play "We Wish You a Merry Christmas." She grinned like an idiot when everyone, even Annette, joined in. The power came back on as she strummed through the final chords and everyone cheered.

Annette touched Toni's hand gently and moved her mouth like she wanted desperately to say something. Toni leaned in slightly. "Did I miss one?"

The girl nodded and pulled Toni close enough to whisper three little words in her ear. Toni thought for a second about the chords and nodded. "I'm not sure I remember all the words. Are you going to help me?"

Annette smiled brightly as she nodded, and Toni began to play one last song for the night. At first, her voice was quiet and tenuous as "O Holy Night" began, but as she let the song fill her up, Annette's voice rang true and clear through the night. Toni watched the girl for a moment, but the joy on Denita's face was so pure that Toni felt tears welling up in her own eyes too. As the song finished, Annette took a small bow and promptly hid behind her father, clenching and unclenching her fists as everyone clapped.

Toni set down her guitar and smiled brightly at Annette. "That was beautiful. Maybe we can do that again sometime."

Annette didn't answer her or even look at her, but Toni knew it wasn't a slight. Denita opened her mouth as if to explain and Toni shook her head. "No worries, Mama. I swear, I get it."

"Sibling?"

"No. But I've done a lot of travelling and made a lot of observations."

"You *are* an angel, I hope you know that." Denita pulled Toni into a hug. "I can't ever thank you enough. It's such a shame we'll forget all of this when we go home."

"What?" Toni asked.

Denita pursed her lips slightly before beginning. "I was born here. I lived here until I was twelve and loved every minute of it. My mom and I left when my dad died. As soon as we left, it was like none of it ever happened at all. I could remember learning things, getting older, some vague recollections of the people I'd known, but that was it. My early childhood, even my dad, all of it was pretty much a blur. I couldn't remember the house we'd lived in or my first dog."

"But you're here now?"

"Entirely by accident, I assure you. We were on our way home from my mother's funeral." Tears filled Denita's eyes.

Toni touched her shoulder. "I'm so sorry for your loss."

"Thank you." She smiled through the tears. "I think Mama wanted to be buried with my dad. We had her ashes with us in the car, driving home. The gas light came on and we took the next exit and here we are. A little like fate. As soon as we came into town, I knew exactly where I was and what had happened. I remember being little. I remember my dad. And now this. This is the best Christmas I've ever had in my life and I'm going to forget it all over again."

"There's a lot I don't understand about this place, about what happens here, but I know this," Toni said. "Even if you forget everything that happened again, it doesn't change that it happened. When do you leave?"

"What?"

"Are you staying through until Christmas?"

"No, we can't. Chris's family is expecting us, and I can't keep Annette from them. She needs all the family she has."

"Don't leave today. Stay at least until tomorrow." Toni yawned deeply. "I've got to get a little sleep but promise me you won't leave today."

"Okay," Denita promised, but looked like she really wanted to ask questions.

Toni said goodnight to Annette and left the room. It did not surprise her in the least to find Vor and Syn standing beside her door, waiting for her.

"That was a beautiful thing you did tonight," Vor said.

"I wanted to help."

"And you definitely did that."

"Well, maybe you can help me do one better. Is there anywhere in town here that would carry a guitar, used or otherwise? Especially one that might be a little on the smaller side?"

Syn thought for a minute before answering. "Why don't you get some sleep. I'll make a few calls and let you know after breakfast."

"Thanks so much." Toni hugged them both before realizing she'd done so. It was too awkward to apologize for being awkward and, really, she didn't get the feeling from them that they thought it was odd at all.

As she packed away her guitar, Toni heard a soft clicking against her window. She knew before she pushed aside the curtain that she'd find the big raven hopping in the snow on the sill, waiting for her. She cranked open the window, but the bird did not come in this time.

"I know you have better things to do than to check up on me, Mr. Raven." He didn't say anything but cocked his head to pierce her with his bright gaze. "Yeah, yeah. Whatever. You go on and tell your lady that all is well and the power is back on. We're safe and sound."

She fished a plain nut from the bowl on the table and a strip of dried meat from the bag on the dresser and set it in front of the big bird before shutting the window. Toni was asleep before she had time to obsess over anything more, but she dreamed of forgetting, of little girls singing, and of her parents.

***

When Toni woke up, it was light out, the bird was gone, and a small guitar case sat leaning up against the dresser. She smiled like a little kid on Christmas morning as she sprang up to see the guitar inside the blank black case. It was a good size to learn on, small enough for tiny fingers but big enough to have some room to grow. It was about as perfect as she could have asked for, but it needed a few more things before she could give it to Annette.

She moved a little faster than she might have otherwise, opting for a quick scrub, a pony tail, and tinted moisturizer that smelled like a milk and orange ice cream bar. Vor was waiting for her at the bottom of the stairs with a secretive smile. "Will that work?"

"It's almost perfect." Toni grinned at her. "I'm going to run over to my truck and get my box and an old DVD that helped me learn to play."

"What's in the box?"

Toni shook her head and put her finger to her lips. "It's a secret," she whispered.

Vor laughed brightly. "I think there's a few rolls left, and I can toss an egg and some ham in a pan, make you a sandwich if you want."

She almost said no. Almost. Before the gleeful light in Vor's eyes could fade, Toni switched it up and brought it back. "You know what? That would be really great."

With a belly full of sandwich and sloshing with some excellent coffee, thanks to her new favorite barista, Nana of Teas Me fame, Toni hurried to Kevin's Garage where her truck sat waiting for its parts to arrive. She knocked on the door but didn't get an answer, so she went around the side where the garage door was rolled up and two men were working under the hood of a newer Honda. "Excuse me." she called over the noise of the shop.

Kevin glanced up and grinned broadly at her. "Glad you came by. It's looking like I'll have your truck all set by Christmas Eve. Your radiator is on its way and should be here in a few days."

"That's great news." And it really should have been, but it didn't really feel like it was, and that was a mess of revelation in her gut. For a moment, she thought about asking him how he managed that but decided that she probably didn't want to know. "I need to get a box out of the back."

"I'm a little greasy at the moment, but the key is on a hook in the office, by the light switches through that door. Try and put it back on the same hook if you would so I don't lose it."

"No problem." She made her way through the garage to the office door. Her key was on the fourth hook in a row of about twelve, most of which had other keys hanging on them. It took her a few minutes to dig out her paints. Maybe it was true; maybe they wouldn't remember their time in Bear Ridge or ever make it back again, but Toni was determined that Annette would remember how it felt in that moment, to be in the spotlight, to be praised for the skills that made her special. She made certain to put the key back on that same fourth hook before high tailing it back to the inn.

Toni took the box to her room and dug out her travel mug. She was going to require coffee and time for this part. After filling her cup from the communal coffee pot in the kitchen, Toni settled in with the blank slate case and her paints, plopped her headphones on, and got to work. The dulcet tones of Halestorm filled her head as she put brush to the black hard shell and worked with the sort of determination she rarely felt anymore.

She didn't know how long she'd been working. Her arms were streaked with acrylic paint, her coffee was gone, and her stomach was complaining. Loudly. But she was nearly finished. If she'd had more time, she would have painted the guitar instead of the case, but she was still happy with the final result. The realization dawned on her that she hadn't given a single thought to where she could spray it down with sealant.

Toni plucked her headphones off her head and stopped her MP3 player only to discover that she had an audience. Large as life, the bane of her current existence and tormenter of her dreams was perched on the chair near the door with a huge grin on his face. "You're really a multitalented sort of woman, aren't you?"

"It seems that you've got some hidden skills yourself. Did you pick the lock?"

"Actually, Syn let me in when we couldn't get your attention. It was a little concerning after a solid five minutes of pounding and yelling."

Toni felt the blush come over her, from the tips of her ears down. "Damn. I'm sorry. I guess I didn't realize how loud the music was."

She noted that she wasn't the least bit upset at Syn for unlocking the door or at Nico for making himself at home in her space instead of letting her know he was there. In fact, she was appreciative. That was both weird and disconcerting.

"It really is beautiful work."

"I wanted her to have something that would at least bring back the smile on her face this morning." She spun on the stool to look at Nico. "I suppose you're a little lost."

Nico shook his head. "Syn filled me in. She and Vor are ridiculously proud of you, by the way."

Toni smiled. It'd been a long time—since her parents died, really—that anyone had been proud of her. Other than herself anyway. The Toni who arrived in Bear Ridge would have brushed it off, but now she wouldn't diminish her favorite women in that way. Toni looked at what she'd created and felt the warmth and satisfaction of a job well done. She'd painted pieces of the town. The gazebo at the park, Max's old Victorian, the inn, the stately old town hall. And she'd painted a bell, her personal signature, in the lower corner beside the words: "My music speaks when I cannot."

"You make stuff?" Toni stared at him, remembering the dragon.

"I do actually, yes," he said with slight confusion.

Toni shook her head and started gesticulating with her hands in big sweeping motions. "I mean you probably have somewhere or know somewhere I can use to spray it down with sealant."

"I do in fact have somewhere you can do that. But it is at my home."

"Whatever. I'm not... I need to get this finished for her." She blushed again and tried to shield her face from his view. "Besides, I wouldn't mind seeing Juni again before I go."

And just like that, the mood changed, the temperature in the room dropping several degrees. "Before you go?"

"Kevin said my truck will be done by Christmas Eve." She tried not to notice the change, not to acknowledge it in any way. "This place is wonderful—it's actually pretty damned amazing—but I have places I'm supposed to be."

"I thought you weren't going anywhere in particular."

"Not for Christmas. I don't do Christmas, except for frightened little girls. I *do* however do New Year's Eve and I'm supposed to be at a dive bar in a suburb of Seattle for their New Year's Eve party."

"Huh." He didn't have any more to say about that. "We should get over to my workshop so you can get this sealed and dried."

"I don't think we have time for that, not really."

"Let's try it and see before you count it out."

"You know what? I'm not even going to argue with you on that." She smiled and picked up the finished case, leaving the guitar safely on her bed.

The ride was a little quieter than Toni had expected. She felt bad, but she'd told him from the start that she wasn't the settling kind of girl. What did he expect? A few dates would change her whole life? The trees got a lot denser as they left the main part of town where the buildings were pretty close together. It was a little silly, but any time she was a passenger driving through thick forests, she watched, waiting to see the faces of the ancient people staring at her from the shadows, faces full of paint and all the knowledge in the world. Once, when she was little, she'd been absolutely certain she'd seen exactly that.

Nico pulled off the road and down a narrower road that she hoped was a driveway. The house it led to was not what she was expecting. She expected a manly, roughhewn, log-cabin type house. This was more retro-modern, '70s inspired aesthetic, like a smaller cousin of Falling Water. "Is this yours?" she asked.

"Yep. I designed it myself."

She felt her jaw drop. "You can't be serious. This is beautiful work."

"Thank you. I like it. I'll take you for a tour when the case is out of the box."

"The box?"

"It's not much more complicated than a hair dryer on a rotary fan. More or less. I like to tinker with things." He stopped the truck in front of a large barn. "I've got to let Juni out, so you might want to prepare for fifty pounds of flying pibble."

"No problem. I really do love dogs, though I've never been able to have one of my own." She got out of the truck and waited patiently for the blur of blue and was not disappointed as Nico opened the door and, save for a brief pause to do her thing, Juniper had a one-track mind for Toni. She wasn't sure she'd ever met anyone so damn happy to see her, let alone one she'd barely missed hitting with her truck.

After both dog and girl had calmed down a bit, Toni got the case out of the truck and followed Nico into the barn, which only looked like a barn on the outside. Inside, it was a workshop. Part of it seemed to be dedicated to the metal working, like the beautiful copper dragon in front of Max's house, another part held a standard workbench, a huge lathe, and an air compressor among a bunch of tools that Toni couldn't identify in the first place. The scent of grease, sawdust, and metal filled the space.

Nico motioned her to a door off to the side. "This is the paint booth. I've got respirators and whatever else you need."

"Wow." She stared at the setup and felt a pang of envy. "There's nothing you can't make in this place, is there? Your setup is amazing."

"It helps that I have the space." He smiled tightly.

Toni set the case on the clean table in the paint booth and walked back over to where Nico stood. She put her hands on either side of his face, deciding to address the heavy atmosphere she couldn't seem to ignore. "I wish I could be the person you want me to be, Nico, I do. But I'm not and I don't know how to be that person. I never meant to mislead you in any way. I've really enjoyed what time we've spent together, and I appreciate your letting me use your space, but I think maybe after today, we should part ways and be done with it. I don't want to hurt you."

He sighed and tilted his head until his forehead touched hers. "I'm sorry I'm not better at keeping everything I'm feeling hidden or at least out of the way. I can't lie to you, though. What I feel for you is stronger than anything I've ever felt before in my life."

"I wish I could be who you want me to be." She closed her eyes, relishing their closeness.

"That's just it, Toni. You already are exactly who I want you to be. I wouldn't change a thing about you. And if that means you'll leave when you're done, then that's what it means, and I need to be the one to remember that. I understand that you're going to leave, and I want whatever time you'll give me. You may not remember our time together, but I will, and I'll treasure it for as long as I live." He pressed his lips to hers.

For a moment, it was as if time stood still. The earth moved, the stars grew brighter, colors everywhere grew more vivid and amazing, but they were in their own bubble, and nothing mattered but his lips on hers.

Instead of pulling away like she should have, Toni leaned in to the kiss, to the man, her whole body singing beneath his fingers. She was no stranger to attraction, but nothing, nothing had ever felt quite like this.

"Hold on." She stepped back from him, as hard as it was to do.

"What?" Nico stared at her incredulously.

"I have to get this sprayed. We can pick up right here in a few minutes. That way, it'll actually have a chance at being dry in time to give it to Annette."

"Annette?"

"That's the girl's name."

Nico nodded. "You're not wrong. I'll get the respirators. There're a few cans of sealant on the shelves over there. Pick your poison and we'll get this wrapped up lickety split."

Toni walked over to the shelf on shaky legs and located a can of spray sealant that would do exactly what she needed, even if she technically needed more time for it to dry than she really had. The actual spraying part didn't take much time at all and Nico loaded the case into his odd box contraption that he'd rigged up to help speed up drying times with heat.

"We shouldn't go far or leave it unattended really." He stepped cautiously toward her, wishing he'd listened to his stupid brother and put a couch in the workshop.

"I'm sure we can figure out something to do while we wait right here." She reached out to take his hand in hers. "But only if we're on the same page. I don't want to hurt you."

"It's already too late for that, I think. I can't bring myself to care about that right now, though. I should have listened to my brother and put a couch in here." He pressed his lips to hers a little more urgently, his tongue tentatively requesting entrance.

Toni followed his lead, leaning in, opening up and letting everything else fall away. Tomorrow didn't matter. It was only them, alone together in that moment. When he touched her, every nerve ending she had shuddered in anticipation. Toni wanted to sit there, on the floor of his workshop, kissing him for as long as she could. His hand slipped under her shirt, feathering over her belly to cup her breast. His thumb skimmed her nipple through her bra and she moaned and arched her back slightly, pressing against him.

A ding sounded somewhere far away, and Nico pulled back. Toni's body followed him of its own volition, seeking his warmth and not finding it. Toni sighed, a little disappointed at the interruption, but understanding that whatever made the ding probably needed to be checked on. His sudden absence left her a bit colder than she wanted to admit.

"It looks like the tour is going to have to wait. The dryer will be done in a bit and I'll take you back over to the inn when it is." Nico offered a hand to help her up. "My brother is headed this way to pick up a few things."

"Oh." She couldn't help but feel disappointed.

Nico smiled. "Glad we're on the same page on that one. We'll get there. Believe me, the wait will be worth it. Promise." He kissed her thoroughly and stepped away. "Keep an eye on that dryer, would you? I have to get Grey's present for Daisy from the house."

"What am I watching for?"

"Mostly electrical issues. If something sparks or smokes, come out and yell. I'm not completely comfortable with how the dryer is set up. I need to redo it eventually, but I've never seen the need until now. I'll be back in a few minutes."

***

When Nico dropped her off at the Bear Ridge Inn, he kept her for a moment with his kiss. She didn't want to leave. She didn't want to get out of the car. She didn't want to be apart anymore, but he had things to do and he'd made that as clear as she'd made the fact that she was leaving.

With a wave, Toni bounced into the inn, up the stairs, and into her room. She put the guitar back in its case and, quite pleased with her handiwork, headed down the hall. Toni knocked on the little family's door and couldn't help but smile when Annette opened the door. "You're exactly who I wanted to see."

Annette looked at her with her big dark eyes, clutching her stuffed bunny tight to her chest. The family had their suitcases packed and organized in the center of the room.

"I have something special for you."

"You've already done so much, Toni." Denita opened the door wider and ushered Toni into the room.

"I actually can't take all the credit on this. Vor and Syn found the guitar, but I painted it so even if you forget everything, you can still remember." Toni pointed out all the town's sites and the little bell that was her signature. "Inside, there are a couple of picks and the DVD that I used to help me learn when I wasn't much older than you. Well, it was on VHS then, but I sort of doubt you've got a VCR on hand."

Annette looked at the guitar with something like reverence as she touched one of the strings. Toni helped her take it out of the case and showed her how to hold it. "It'll take a while before it sounds like music, but I'm betting that you have patience to spare when you want to, when it's something that matters to you."

Annette didn't look at her, but she was smiling as she plucked at the strings and made it ring.

"If you look, and she is willing, you should be able to find a teacher if the DVD or the Internet aren't enough." Toni stood up and walked toward the door. "I hope you all have a really safe trip home and a merry Christmas."

"Thank you so much." Denita hugged her tight. "I hope we meet again someday."

"Me too." Toni found herself hugging the woman back before escaping to her room to try not to obsess over all that happened and everything that would never happen. It was a hard place to be and it made her feel too many things at once. It was not a comfortable feeling, like there was no way to make the right choice.

Chapter Six

The next day, after the best night's sleep she'd had in a while, Toni got her few chores done early, as Jo had sent her a message about lunch with the girls. Moving as much as she did, it had been a long time since Toni had hung out with anyone, let alone a group of people with whom she clicked. She was dressed simply but warmly with the barest of makeup and her hair in a neat and tidy pony. She was ready to go by the time Jo and Wohpe arrived in a large van filled to the brim with plastic totes and foil trays.

"What's the plan for today?" Toni climbed up in the van in the open seat behind Wohpe.

"First, we have a few deliveries to make. At least once a week, we take a hot lunch and supplies out to some of our residents who don't get around so well, and it's our turn for delivery. Then we'll meet up with the rest of girls in the park." Jo pulled easily into what seemed like actual traffic in town. "Don't worry, we aren't the only ones working though. Daisy, Krissy, and Melanie are on scrub detail."

"Scrub detail?"

"With the new baby and everything, Jen and Bran need a little extra help on chores right now so they're cleaning and cooking and whatever Jen needs for the morning."

"That's really awesome. You guys do this every week?"

"No. We do this once a month." Wohpe turned in her seat to face Toni better. "We have a rotation. Next week it'll be another group. It's all volunteer—it's not like you have to do these things."

"It's one of those small-town amazing things, then?"

"You don't do that in your town?"

"I've not really had a town in years, and when I did, we weren't really around much."

"That's right. Jo said something about you living in your truck. I can't even imagine that. Where do you put your things? Do you have a storage thingy somewhere?"

Toni laughed. "No. I really don't have stuff the way I used to. When I was little, my parents and I had a house and the usual sorts of things, but we weren't ever there. Every weekend, every vacation, we were gone. Honestly, I have enough clothes. I have a big trunk I use as a bench or a table in the truck that's long-term storage, and my pack for everything else. I really don't need a whole lot. I travel light."

"I think light is an understatement." Jo laughed and shook her head. "Okay, we're at the first of the deliveries. Honestly, there aren't as many houses during the warmer months, but some people should not be out and about when the roads are bad. Mabel, our first stop, she's more than capable of taking care of herself for the most part, but I swear she looks like one bad tumble will shatter everything. She looks like a tiny little fairy."

"But she's not," Wohpe assured her, as if Toni might believe she actually was one. "She *was* a ballerina once upon a time, though. To hear her tell it, she was pretty famous in the town she grew up in."

It took them two hours to deliver thirteen meals. It wouldn't have taken as long if each stop hadn't come with a story and a few words and, in one, Toni was able to fix a toilet that wouldn't stop running. It was nice to feel useful and do something good for someone else beyond being kind and polite. Everyone had been grateful for the company more than anything. Except Paul—he'd been happiest not to have to listen to that hissy watery sound of the running toilet.

With the deliveries finished, they headed toward the park where they were meeting the others. Wohpe had gotten in the now empty back part of the van to sit with Toni, clearly anxious to talk about something a little more personal. "I'm going to stick my nose where it doesn't belong now."

"I figured." Toni tried to smile but figured it looked as strangely grimaced as it felt.

"I love Nico, no doubt, but like a brother. I know you've made it crystal clear to him that you're leaving, and that he said he doesn't care... but I'm asking you not to hurt him too badly."

"I don't want to hurt anybody." Toni grew quiet, sort of wishing for Wohpe to go back to her initial opinion, that Nico needed a little fun in his life. Toni didn't want these women to think less or poorly of her. She couldn't remember the last time she'd cared what someone thought.

"I know. I'm a little worried about you too. I don't want you to get hurt either and, right now, it's looking like this is going to end with both of you hurting." She pursed her lips together like she wanted to say more.

Toni sighed. "Are you going to try and get me to stay as well?"

Wohpe shook her head. "No. That's the kind of thing no one should do, only you can make that decision and that's how it should be. I'll be perfectly honest with you, Toni, I didn't expect to like you at all when Nico told me about you—but only because I hate to see him get hurt. I think I might be more upset that I like you too because I know you're leaving when your truck is done and I've enjoyed spending time with you. Plus, you know how to fix a toilet. Which is pretty amazing considering I have no clue how to do that and I have two of them in my house and you have none in your truck. How the hell did you know how to do that, anyway?"

She snorted, happy Wohpe took the conversation in a different direction. "My Dad taught me that kind of stuff growing up. He did all sorts of odd jobs and I was his helper in the summers when he had to work. I learned a lot."

"You might fit in here better than we thought." Wohpe laughed. "You did not have what one would call a normal childhood, did you?"

"Yeah, no. Definitely not."

"It sounds like you had a marvelous adventure though."

"I did." Toni looked at Wohpe strangely. "I know it was unconventional, but I wouldn't have changed it for anything."

"I don't think you understand my point... I love Bear Ridge, but it is insular, and people have a lot of expectations that go unmet, leading to great disappointment and an inability to enjoy the things they *do* have right in front of them. It's amazing you've gotten to see so much and go to so many places, as young as you are."

"I was a lucky kid." Toni spoke with a decisive tone that made it clear that part of the conversation was over.

They were quiet for a few minutes before Wohpe asked, "Have you ever built a snowman?" An excited smile spread over her face.

Toni furrowed her brow in thought for a moment. "You know what, I don't think I have."

"Ha. I know what we're going to do today. Jo." Wohpe reached under the bench seat and pulled out a box, digging through it for a moment before shrieking victoriously and dropping a pair of thick mittens on Toni's lap and matching three other sets.

Jo parked on the edge of the park and grabbed a pair of mittens for herself. "If you've never built a snowman, I don't imagine you've ever had a snowball fight either."

"You'd be right." Toni nodded.

"I take it back, I vote snowball fight. Everyone should have at least one snowball fight with friends. We have a little time before the others get here to get ready. We'll make it fair though and set them up a little bit too." Wohpe grinned.

"Is this something you guys do a lot?" Toni pulled the mittens on and followed them out into the snow, lamenting her lack of good winter boots. She'd never really bothered with snow much before and definitely wasn't prepared for it. "What do I do exactly?"

"Take a bunch of snow in your hands and press it together into a ball. It's pretty much that simple." Jo grinned, and instead of putting her snowball into a pile, she chucked it right at Toni, hitting her square the chest.

"Oh." Toni shook her head in indignation and started gathering snow and hurling it. She darted behind bushes and trees to avoid the coming snow and sent her own white missiles toward Wohpe and Jo and then Daisy, Melanie, and Krissy too as they arrived and joined the game without any hesitation. She ran through the playground, leaping from side to side to avoid the snowballs headed her direction and threw others back at the girls. Hiding behind the big slide, Toni took a deep breath and realized she couldn't remember the last time she'd had so much fun. She busted out laughing as Wohpe took a snowball to the gut and Daisy got nailed in the shoulder, then Melanie tripped over something and ended up on her back, laughing as she made a snow angel.

The six of them, after warming up at Teas Me over some ridiculously good coffee and hot chocolate, headed to the Health Center where Toni had been rushed after her accident. There were four people in residence there apart from Dr. Cait and his nurse, Gina Stark. At first, Toni felt a little out of place singing Christmas carols to strangers, but with her new friends, it all came so easy. Her voice fit in nicely with the others, finding a place in the lower ranges where she could be a part of—and not the star—of the song. It was a new and strange place for her to be, but she enjoyed it thoroughly.

"I can't thank you girls enough for bringing a bit of cheer." Dr. Cait shook their hands. Something about him reminded Toni of a wild animal. He looked like he'd be more at one with the woods and herbs and poultices than he did with a pristine white coat and the stethoscope around his neck. "And you are looking well, Miss Bell."

"Thanks to you." Toni took the hand he offered. "You did a wonderful job patching me up."

"I'm glad I could help." He looked at her appraisingly. "Have you been having fun in our little town while waiting on your truck?"

"I really have. It's an unforgettable place." Toni nearly stepped back at the round of laughter that erupted from everyone in the room. "Guys, you don't honestly buy into that crap, do you?"

Dr. Cait lifted his hands up in the air. "I do understand your reluctance to believe a lot of things. I would say that you'll find out, but really, when you leave, you'll remember none of this. So, ultimately what does it matter if you believe or not? You can't change the truth of it. I could tell you that you are in the presence of gods, goddesses, myths, and legends and, no matter how true, it won't matter if you believe. The truth doesn't require belief, that's the beauty of it. Some things just are. The Earth is round, time keeps moving, and, in Bear Ridge, magic is real."

Toni wanted to scoff, to react, but something he said made a few things click in her head and she couldn't help but wonder if *maybe*. She shook her head and tried to make that thought go right out her ear again. "Nope. Not today, Doctor Cait. I appreciate your help and your expertise, but I'm not dealing with metaphysical, mystical, magical whizzbang today."

He looked at her and laughed. "I'm sure I'll be seeing you around again one of these days."

"I do tend to keep running into people here, so there's a possibility." She turned to the girls again. "What's next on the agenda for the day?"

"The service portion of our day is at an end. Usually we celebrate with dinner. You are more than welcome to join us." Jo grabbed Toni's hand in hers. "There's a mostly okay pizza place we like. The crust is a little thin and the sauce is a little punchy, but we like it fine, especially with friends."

This time, Toni didn't hesitate at all. "Sounds perfect to me."

They all piled in Jo's van and Daisy's happy little yellow car and headed toward the pizza place. It was bigger than Toni was expecting, built around the centerpiece of great brick pizza ovens. They had a warm, welcoming atmosphere and a big bald dude in white twirling dough behind the long counter. The girls all crowded around a large, round table, ordering a pitcher of both beer and soda, and three large pizzas: a veggie, a meat lover's, and a four-cheese pizza.

Toni ended up between Jo and Daisy and across from Wohpe. She turned to Daisy who was again wearing yellow. It was a great color for her, but she'd never seen so many different yellow outfits maybe ever. "You have a thing for the color yellow like I do purple."

"It's my favorite. It's such a happy color," Daisy said. "I know most people aren't really into it quite the way I am but…"

"From what I can see, it suits you. You seem to me to be about as happy as yellow."

Daisy looked at her strangely for a second before her smile got even bigger. "I think that's the most interesting compliment I've ever received. Thank you."

"Only passing along the truth, really."

"Well, I'm going to return the favor a little bit, even if you don't want me to." Daisy took Toni's hand in hers. "I mean the passing along of the truth bit—not the weird compliment bit. I like you and all, but I don't know that I can do weird compliments like you did. It'd take me all day to think of one. Sorry. I'm rambling. The truth thing though. I think you are discounting a lot of things you've seen because of how you were raised. I feel like maybe, for all your amazing travels, you didn't get to witness a lot of the magic in your childhood. Or maybe you got to see too much of it. For whatever reason, I think you're immune or blind to it now. Maybe think about it a little."

"Um. Okay." Toni didn't know how best to respond to her, or how to respond at all, actually. She decided she was going to accept the comment without comment. Bear Ridge was an amazing place, no doubt, but magic? How could magic be a real thing with all the terrible things going on in the world?

Whatever she might have said or thought flitted away with the arrival of the pizzas and subsequent feasting. It took no time at all to get caught up in the comradery of the night. They laughed together, poked fun at each other, and enjoyed each other's company. Toni couldn't remember ever having a group of girlfriends to hang out with. She made friends easily enough but only for a weekend at a time. It was something very different to have friends who stopped by for the hell of it to rope you in to volunteering and still turned it into one of the best days she'd had in a long time. If she wasn't careful, it wasn't only Nico she was going to miss when she left. As much fun as she was having, Toni was acutely aware how complicated it was getting.

Chapter Seven

Toni stared at the ceiling, annoyed at not being able to fall asleep. It was a beautiful room, she was neither too warm or too cold, the bed was comfortable, she was even tired—but no. Sleep was a thing that she was not going to be able to do. She rolled and tossed for a moment before completely giving up the ghost.

Food might be exactly the thing she needed. The making of it more than the eating of it. Maybe Vor wouldn't mind having a day off.

Toni pulled on her comfortable old sweats and headed quietly for the kitchen. It was two in the morning and she didn't need to be waking up other people. When she reached the dining room, Toni distinctly heard the sounds of someone singing Christmas carols. Curious, she peeked into the beautifully appointed kitchen only to find Vor dancing around the big marble-topped island as she mixed something in a large bowl.

"Couldn't sleep either?" Toni smiled as she stepped into the kitchen.

Vor nearly dropped the mixing bowl but recovered well. "I hope I'm not keeping you up."

"Not even a little. I came down because I was having a hard time sleeping and cooking helps. It's been a long time since I had access to a real kitchen." She eyed the bowl in Vor's arms. "What are you making?"

"I always make a truckload of cookies for wherever the trucks are going."

"What?"

"Every so often, I'll get the word from a particular individual who knows things that maybe they shouldn't know about a truck passing through Bear Ridge, usually on the way to deliver interesting things to places with children. When that happens, I make sure that truck, or those trucks, depending, have enough cookies too."

Toni stared at her.

"I know, I know. There's nothing any of us can do to make you believe until you do." She laughed. "Come on, if you want to bake, help me with cookies. I've got the sugar cookies started here if you want to do some chocolate chip or some allergy-friendly cookies."

"I wouldn't trust myself on anything for kids with allergies, so I'll do the chocolate chip. Maybe when I'm done with those, you'll let me add a batch of my childhood favorites."

"What would that be?"

"Snickerdoodles of course."

"It's been a few years since I've done those. That'd be perfect." Vor smiled brightly. "I can't remember the last time I had company on a baking night."

"Syn doesn't help?"

Vor laughed, a deep rolling belly laugh. "Only if I want to have half the cookies burnt and the other half raw. Oh, I love her, and she really does try, but some people should not be allowed to touch anything that requires ingredients."

"I promise I can bake a passable cookie." Toni laughed and got to work on the chocolate chip cookies, gathering up the ingredients and measuring and weighing before mixing. They didn't say much at first, content to share the space and exist together for a bit. It wasn't until she was rolling little dough balls in cinnamon and sugar for snickerdoodles that Toni found herself talking, in part because there was a friendly ear available and maybe because she really hadn't before.

"When we first moved into a place with a real oven and not a camp stove, my mom tried to make real cookies from scratch from an old recipe of her mother's that she'd kept in her scrapbook," Toni said, lost in memory. "The recipe said oleo and we walked the aisles at the grocery store for what felt like eternity trying to find oleo. We didn't have the Internet and the stock boy had never heard of it before. We ended up making chocolate chip cookies with the recipe on the bag instead. It was years before I found out that oleo is margarine. I think that was the only time she made cookies." Toni cracked the eggs like a pro.

"Where did you learn to bake then?" Vor asked.

"My dad." She smiled thinking of him. "He didn't know what oleo was either, but he had heck of a sweet tooth and was the most frugal person I've ever known so he baked when we were at the house to take with us when we were on the road. I'd sit in the back and read whatever book I'd gotten from the library that week, munching on whatever amazing thing he'd made for the trip."

"That sounds lovely."

"It was. I haven't really baked anything in years. It makes me think of my dad." Toni stirred the chocolate chips into the bowl. "My mom was amazing at other things. She could make something out of nothing in no time flat and somehow get people to pay her for it. She'd set up on the beach while my dad and I were playing in the water and draw people or paint sea shells for souvenirs. I was with her the first time I sold a painting of my own, a watercolor landscape I probably would have thrown out, but I got thirty bucks for it because she put it up on the line with her own work."

"How long have they been gone now?" Vor asked.

"Almost a decade. At least they went together. That's how they would have wanted it." Toni slid two trays in one of the ovens and perched on a stool. "They wanted to see every beach, every campground in the world. They managed a good number of them before I came along and tossed a wrench in the plans."

"I doubt they felt that way." Vor put a hand on Toni's shoulder.

"I know they loved me… but they hated that house, their office jobs, the idea of the PTA and HOA. My mom always said if she'd had the patience, she'd have homeschooled me and kept on travelling." Toni found herself jumping from memory to memory, some of which she kept to herself, some she shared, but it was cathartic to have someone willing to listen.

"Who taught you music?" Vor asked as they put one of the batches of cookies on the cooling racks. "You got your art from your mom, your handiness from your dad—where'd the music come from?"

"It was the Christmas I was ten. We were at some little town in Texas on the Gulf of Mexico and there was a busker who amazed me. I wanted to sit and listen to him all day. It's the only time I remember asking for something for Christmas. We didn't really do the whole presents thing—my parents really *were* staunch minimalists," she said with a smile. "They took me to a pawn shop the day after Christmas to pick it out." Toni felt the tears welling up and tried to wipe them away before they could fall.

"Honey, you need to let it out. Don't bottle that all up again." Vor wrapped Toni up in her arms, allowing her to find the safety to cry for her parents for the first time in years. She cried until there was nothing left inside her, until she could barely stand.

Vor led her back to the blue room and tucked her into the big empty bed with sweet words and a kiss on the forehead before shutting off the lights, leaving the little tree twinkling on the table for company before shutting the door behind her.

***

Toni woke up a little after one in the afternoon feeling drained but more open than she had in years. Vor made her want to believe in magic, in Bear Ridge. If she were completely honest with herself, so did Nico. His silly earnest profession of love, even if he didn't quite say it that way, warmed parts of her heart that she had thought were long since dead and beyond resuscitation.

She washed and dressed in jeans and a gray sweater with threads of silver throughout it, a subtle sparkle to match the subtle sparkle in her metallic gray eyeshadow. No one else might notice it, but it made her happy to shine a little. And if she was a tiny bit liberal with her glitter, it wouldn't matter to anyone who mattered.

When Toni walked into the kitchen, Vor and Syn were busy packing up the cookies into foil trays. "You're just in time. The truck pulled into the diner about ten minutes ago and the driver says he's more than happy to take these cookies to go along with his other packages."

"Seriously? How will he remember what they're for when he leaves?"

"Scoff all you want." Vor waved her off. "Honestly, we don't know if any of the cookies go where they're meant to go, and maybe it doesn't matter really. Somebody is going to enjoy the cookies— we hope it's someone who needs a moment of happiness, but it really doesn't matter, does it?"

"But no one ever gets to say thank you."

Syn and Vor looked at each other for a moment, and a small secret smile passed between them. "You're right. No one says thank you for the cookies, but if we only did things for a thank you, then that would be more about us than them, wouldn't it? Did you bake last night for a thank you?"

"Well… no, but…"

Vor smiled at her. "Dear child, I think you understand fine."

"I do, but there's really something to be said for the bright shining faces. Yesterday I went with Jo and the girls on their monthly volunteering outing and it was great fun and I felt accomplished at the end of the day. That said, my favorite part was still the look on Paul's face when I fixed his toilet."

"But the day would have been no less rewarding if you hadn't gotten to see that."

"I get what you're saying. I guess I'm not quite at that level of magnanimous yet. Maybe when I'm your age."

Both Vor and Syn laughed like Toni made the best joke they'd ever heard.

"What?"

"The other day, before I got called away to help deliver the baby, we were going to have a conversation. I think maybe now is the time." Syn motioned to an empty chair. "The armor you found in the basement isn't a prop for any sort of stage or party or holiday. It's not for display. Hell, I don't remember the last time anyone has seen it. We used to wear it all the time."

"For what?" Toni stared at them. "I think you'd better say what you want to say here."

"The armor is standard dress for the place we come from." Vor took a deep breath. "Many, many years ago, Syn and I lived a different kind of life. We lived in a place far away and very separate from here. Our people changed, our warriors no longer believed, and our power diminished. We were never considered particularly important goddesses in our time, not even given the rank of Valkyrie by some scholars. At least I wasn't. Syn is usually listed. We left Valhalla two hundred years ago when there was some upheaval there. It didn't take us long to find ourselves here in Bear Ridge."

Toni stared at her. And stared some more. "You can't expect me to believe that. Really."

Sadness washed over Vor's face. "Why not?"

"You're telling me that the two of you are hundreds of years old."

"Thousands," Syn corrected her.

"Because that's even more believable." Toni shoved her hands through her hair, making a mess of it as she pulled it a little. "So, what the hell can goddesses do anyway? Do you have like, magic powers? Can you heal things? Can you bring things back to life?"

"No. No one but Death deals with death, though deals can be made with him sometimes. There are people here who can heal." Syn touched the place on Toni's forehead that had been a wound a few days earlier. "Have you ever healed so fast before?"

Toni pursed her lips. She hadn't. She couldn't deny that or even pretend she hadn't noticed that it was strange. "So, Doctor Cait is... what? Some Norse God?"

"Celtic." Vor corrected her, like it made any difference at all. "His proper name is Dian Cecht."

"No. You can't be serious. This whole town has been making fun of me all this time. You've all been in cahoots somehow. You made it so my phone doesn't work, and you've been toying with me, trying to make me believe some crazy shit—for what? You think this is funny?" She felt the anger welling up. She'd promise she wouldn't get angry, but she didn't expect them to tell her something so outlandish.

"No, certainly not."

"Then you're all delusional. What the hell is wrong with you?" Toni stood up and hurried out of the kitchen, grabbing her coat from the closet before heading out into the too-bright afternoon. She couldn't believe that they—*they*¬—were a part of this charade. She didn't understand how she could have been so wrong trusting them and letting them into her heart.

She felt the sting of angry tears and quickly blinked them away. Being hurt by Vor and Syn's actions was stupid. And it proved that protecting her heart was the best course. No matter how seemingly wonderful the image was, being alone was safer.

Mr. Raven fluttered down to perch on the lamp and cawed at her.

"Don't start with me. Laugh it up, why don't you? You don't have everyone trying to convince you that they're all some crazy magic people in a crazy magic town." The bird bobbed his head and made a sound like laughter. "That's not nice, you know. I'd even say it's rude."

Toni huffed and started walking down the street. Mr. Raven continued to follow her, nattering and cawing at her. She waved her arms and tried to shoo him away, much to his seeming amusement. Instead of arguing, Toni ran. She didn't exactly know where she was going but it didn't surprise her at all when she ended up in the warm comfort of Teas Me.

"You look like you've had a stressful day, dear. Let me get you something to warm you up."

"Thanks, Nana." Toni sat down at a table after hanging her coat on the back of the chair. "You don't by chance think you're some kind of magic goddess or anything, do you?"

"Oh?" The large woman set a cup of coffee in front of her, adjusted her apron, and smiled. "I don't think that, dear. I know it."

"Not that kind of goddess. You're certainly a goddess, but you're not under some sort of crazy delusion that you're a real *god*-type goddess though." She sipped her coffee and immediately felt a little bit better.

"Toni dear, I imagine you've heard something unbelievable then?"

"My ladies, I mean, the ladies that run the inn, they're trying to convince me that they're some kind of Norse goddesses."

"What would it mean if they were telling you the truth? Really. Think about it. What does it mean to you? You're awfully upset for it to mean nothing, so there must be a reason you're upset." Nana sat down opposite her.

"Everyone here seems to think they're magic. I don't know about the girls I spent yesterday with. I mean, they all seem so normal, so fun, but what if they start spouting this too?"

"What if they do?" Nana smiled at her.

"Magic isn't really real."

"Isn't it?" Nana patted Toni's hand. "Not everyone you've met here in Bear Ridge has magic, but a lot of them do. You don't want to believe and that's fine. We won't hold it against you. You'll reach a point where there will be something you can't rationalize away."

"Life isn't that way, though. There is no magic, no happy ever after."

"That life exists at all is sort of magic though, isn't it?" Nana held a closed hand out to Toni. "You can go through life never knowing any of it, turning your back on it, closing your eyes to it, or you can learn to understand that a little sadness, a little darkness, doesn't negate the good or the light."

As Nana opened her hand, Toni watched open-mouthed as a small point of light bloomed in the center of her palm, expanding to illuminate the entire shop in pale, warm light.

"How did... Who..." words poured from her without her even knowing she was speaking.

"I have many names, like a great many people in this place. I prefer Nana. It feels right." She closed her hand and opened it again. The light was gone, and in its place sat a small round stone with a star inside it. Nana pressed it into Toni's hand. "Someday, you might be in need of a little magic, and now, you'll have it."

"But I won't know I have it, if I believe what I've been told."

"You won't need to know. Magic doesn't need you to know, to believe, or anything. It exists regardless of your opinion." Nana stood up, moved quickly and gracefully back around the counter to fill up a to-go cup with her coffee, snapped a lid on it and set it in front of Toni. "It sounds like you have a lot to think about."

"I know." Toni took the cup in both hands and held it close. "Daisy is your granddaughter, right?"

"Yes."

"Can she do what you do?"

"I don't think she can do the things that I do, she's mostly mortal after all, but I imagine she has a talent or two." Nana took a rag and started wiping the counter down. "I think you should ask her that question, if you really want to know the answer."

"I don't know that I want to know."

"I guess now you know what you should be figuring out."

Toni took the cup and left some money then headed back out into the cold. She knew what she had to do but it was hard. How could she believe the impossible? How could she not believe it after what Nana showed her, gave to her. And she turned around and marched right back into the shop. "What about Nico?"

"Nicodemous can tell you himself. I'm pretty sure he's down at Past Presents. Max had a bit of a snafu with that beautiful dragon he built."

Toni nodded brusquely and headed for the beautiful old Queen Anne. She nearly stopped three times on the way. Once because she was absolutely certain she'd seen something she didn't—couldn't have—seen. No man was actually that big. She'd seen nothing more than a shadow. It had to be. Giants weren't really real. Neither were crazy Celtic gods or Valkyries.

By the time she reached Nico, Toni had herself all worked up again, her mind playing tricks on her at every turn. He was packing his tools into his truck when she got there. He took one look at her and stopped everything. "What happened?"

"You don't already know?" She laughed humorlessly.

"I've been a little busy here."

"You all say this place is magic, that magic people who *don't exist* live here."

"Well, yes, sort of, but they do exist."

"Show me. Show me all the magic."

"I can do that, but not tonight. I know exactly what you need to see." He took her hands in his and pulled her close, wrapping her in his warmth. "Whatever brought this on is enough for one night. Tonight, we're going to relax and not think about anything bigger than you and me and a warm, dark theater."

"What?" She stared at him incredulously.

"They're playing a double feature of classic Christmas movies at the theater tonight. Then tomorrow we'll find you that magic. Say, over a picnic."

"A picnic?" She wanted to argue when she had no right. She wanted to throw a petulant tantrum until he did what she wanted—but she had no real right to ask anything of him.

"Yes. Trust me." He kissed her forehead. "Are you willing to do that? I promise, I'll show you want you want to see, what you need to know."

Unable to trust her own words, she nodded. The answer came too easily for Toni. Something about him turned her brain to mush. She did trust him. She wanted to believe him. She wanted him and that was a whole different kind of mess she both wanted and didn't want.

***

The theater was small but clean and renovated with plush red seats and a large white screen with red curtains on either side. There was a stage surface as well, and Toni realized that the theater probably did live shows too, which was pretty interesting. It wasn't too crowded, with mainly couples making up the audience, leaning in close, huddled over their popcorn and sodas while they watched Danny Kaye and Bing Crosby sing and dance with fans and feathers. It didn't take long to lose herself in the movies and the company. A little zing rushed through her each time Nico's fingers brushed hers as they reached for popcorn.

When he dropped her off at the inn, Toni was about to invite him up when he kissed her. And kept kissing her.

"I'll pick you up at ten. Wear something comfortable." Nico smiled mischievously.

"Okay. Where are we going?"

"If I told you, I'd ruin all the surprises."

"Then give me something to do. Let me help."

"Fine. You can pack lunch. Something light and easy—don't go to any trouble doing it." He pressed his lips to hers again before rushing back to his truck, leaving Toni standing on the porch confused, excited, and already missing him.

Chapter Eight

Toni woke early to shower and get ready, taking a little extra care with her makeup. While part of her was anxious to know what Nico was planning, the louder part was excited for the surprise of it. Toni loved surprises. Well, good surprises anyway. She was going to surprise him right back.

She wanted to feel bad for avoiding Syn and Vor, but she couldn't stop thinking about how they tried to make her believe they were something they couldn't be, how they lied to her. Instead, she made her way to the diner to ask Jo about a deli or a grocery store.

"Toni." Jo grinned at her as she walked into the diner. "How's it going?"

"Pretty well, thanks." She slipped onto a stool at the counter. "I'm in need of a deli."

"A deli?"

"Nico is planning something, and I guess I'm in charge of a picnic."

"How romantic," she said with a saucy grin.

Toni felt herself blush. "I have to admit, I've never made up a picnic before."

"Even better." Jo leaned forward conspiratorially. "I've got a basket you can use, and it won't take me but a minute to throw something together."

"I appreciate that, Jo, I do, but I really sort of want to do this myself. If you're serious about the basket though, that would be great."

"You're so stinking cute. I love it. Hold on a second." Jo disappeared into the kitchen where there was some banging and clanging and at least one dirty word before she reappeared with a large basket in her hands. "Have fun."

"I certainly hope so. Thanks so much."

"No problem." She handed Toni a piece of paper. "Directions to the deli. It's really not that far."

"No worries. It's a really lovely day for December." Toni hooked the basket's handles with her left arm and headed out into the day, feeling a little more like Dorothy than she wanted to.

She made it back to the inn with a full basket and no time to spare. She didn't even get to the door before Nico's truck pulled up to the gate. She turned on her heel and made her way to him. She greeted him with a grin and a lingering kiss, reluctant to pull away. It was hard for her to resist his attraction.

"I have a surprise for you." Nico smiled as he helped her up into his truck. "You're going to love it."

Toni smiled and shook her head. "I hope you like chicken. It's been a long time since I've even been on a picnic, let alone put one together. Like, I think I was maybe nine years old the last time I did, so hopefully I haven't massively screwed it up. Are you sure we're not going to freeze?"

"You've never had a winter picnic before?" he asked.

"Only ever in warm places." She laughed.

"I keep telling you to trust me. One of these days, you will." Nico started up the truck and headed away from the center of town. They drove through a beautiful but quite dark forest dotted with great gray boulders covered with lichens and moss. When the trees grew thinner, the terrain changed, and the dirt looked lighter, almost like sand.

"What the hell?" Toni looked out at the window at a small body of water that looked a lot bigger than it could possibly be. "Did we leave Bear Ridge?"

"No. If we had, you wouldn't remember." He smiled and parked the truck.

She opened the door and the change in the air was immediate. "I smell salt. Seriously?"

Toni was out of the truck before Nico could say anything. The beach itself was at least half a mile long. Part looked to be soft sand and part looked to be rocky, tidepool-pocked beach. It was like nothing she'd ever seen before. She dipped her hand in the water and found it to be cold but far warmer than she expected. And it was definitely salt water.

"What ocean is this?"

"I don't actually know the answer to that." Nico shrugged. "It may not always be the same one."

"This is incredible."

"And this is only the first part of your surprise."

"What?" Toni looked up at him and for the first time noticed the large white canvas tent strewn with shell garlands and tiny fairy lights. "What's this?"

"The perfect place for a picnic." Nico smiled and took her hand in his. "I promised you some magic you could see, didn't I?"

"You did." She smiled up at him. "It's wonderful."

"And you haven't seen the inside yet." He led the way, picnic basket in hand, toward the tent. There was a stone-edged fire pit with a fire ready and waiting to be lit, a large tub of ice with a bottle of champagne, and two purple glass champagne flutes. "I wanted to give you something that would be special."

Toni peeked into the tent at the bed made with crisp blue sheets and a huge down comforter. "You did this for me?"

"And only you." Nico set the basket on the long driftwood bench and knelt down before her, gracefully untying her boots. "I've wanted you since the moment I met you."

"I nearly hit your dog."

"You nearly killed yourself trying to make sure that you didn't." He helped her out of her boots and into the tent, sliding his own shoes off at the entrance.

The tent didn't feel cramped or small; instead it felt cozy and cocoon-like. Toni stared for a moment at the bed, her heart racing at the idea of touching Nico, of pressing herself against him. "There's something about you that gets under my skin, Nico. I don't understand it. It shouldn't be happening this way."

"But it is." He led her toward the bed, setting their coats on a small trunk tucked off to the side. "You're beautiful."

Toni's hands trembled as she reached for him, pressing her lips to his. They sat on the bed, pulling at clothing, rushed fingers tripping over buttons and zippers, only coming apart to remove the barriers between them until they were skin to skin. Her body responded to his in ways that were new and unfamiliar. She was no innocent young girl, but with him, everything was new again.

He paused for a moment, pulling away long enough to put a condom on, for which the usually cautious Toni was grateful as she had completely forgotten to take any precautions.

When he entered her, it was as if time stopped for one perfect moment, pausing in reverence. He fit her as if he'd been made specifically for her, sculpted from living marble. She sighed as he moved with graceful and powerful thrusts as they rocked together, building the connection between them until it exploded in a riot of colors and sensations. For a moment, they rested, catching their breath, holding each other as they recovered. And then they started again. Matching stroke for stroke, peak for peak, as they gave themselves to each other, wholly and completely, until they had nothing left to give.

Lying together, swaddled in down, Toni listened to his heartbeat and memorized the rhythm. No heart would ever sound as strong and pure to her. No arms would ever be so right again. This was not how her life was supposed to go. She was not the sort of woman who settled down with a passel of children, choosing the PTA over the stage or the mosh pit. She didn't do serious relationships. But this time, this one time with this one man, she wanted to. He was so easy to love, to imagine herself growing old with. He was why she had to leave as quickly as possible.

"You're thinking too loudly." Nico pulled her closer and kissed the top of her head. "No more thinking today. I want you to let all that go and be in the moment, be you with me. I would love nothing more than to sit right here in this bed forever, but I've made some special plans today. I believe I have a wish to grant. Now, get dressed. I want to show you something."

"A wish?"

"You asked me to show you magic, didn't you? I didn't spend all morning throwing together a tent and a campfire." Nico handed Toni her panties with a smile. "These are cute."

Toni snatched the purple lace with a roll of her eyes and a flush of her cheeks. It was much colder without a naked Nico lying next to her, so she hurried to get dressed. She was curious to see what his idea of magic would be. Given the afternoon, she couldn't help but have high hopes for the evening.

When she stepped out of the canvas tent, she smiled. He'd set up their lunch beside the now roaring fire in full view of the crashing waves. "I probably should have let Jo put together lunch."

Nico shook his head and pulled her to sit beside him. "No. This is perfect. I like that you put everything together."

"Okay." For a few moments, they busied themselves with their plates, piling them with cold fried chicken and tabbouleh. As they ate, Toni watched the horizon, the crashing waves reaching closer and closer as the tide came in. In the distance, she spotted a tail breaching the surface and slapping the water before disappearing again. "I think it's a dolphin or maybe a small whale." She tried to point it out to Nico, but it was gone and he smiled at her with mischief in his eyes.

As Toni watched, the animal came closer and closer to the shore and soon, it was apparent that it wasn't alone. Toni leapt up and started running for the water. "It's chasing someone. We've got to help."

Nico was close behind but instead of joining her in trying to help, he was holding her, keeping her from diving into the surf. "That's Cheryl, and she isn't in any danger, I promise. She's who I've brought you to see."

Toni stopped struggling and turned to stare at him. "What? She's being chased?"

"No, she's really not. That isn't a dolphin, or a whale or a shark. That tail belongs to her."

"What?" Toni stared out into the water and spotted the tail again, this time only some thirty yards from the shore. The tail flashed again, sort of gray, sort of blue, and speckled with yellow, almost like a queen angelfish in color… but Toni could only see a portion of the fluke and no dorsal fin or pectoral fins. There weren't any pauses for breathing, so it couldn't be any kind of whale, and the colors were wrong for pretty much everything. "Nico, what the hell is this?"

"Cheryl." He smiled at her and took her hand in his. "Please do us all an enormous favor… don't scream."

"*What*?" She no sooner spoke than a woman—or something that sort of looked like a woman—broke the surface of the sea a bit past the breakers. Her flesh was more blue than pink, and her hair was long, nearly white, and tangled with kelp. She lifted her arm and waved at Nico, calling in a strange, trilling voice. Toni could see that there was webbing between her fingers. The impossible became possible. Everything she knew was suddenly completely wrong. "She's a…"

"Say it out loud, you'll feel better." He pulled Toni close to his side.

"She's a *mermaid*," Toni whispered breathlessly.

"Yep, she is."

"Is she a real one or is this like what they do in Florida or some Esther Williams thing?" Toni couldn't help but stare as the woman—fish?—brought herself up onto the shore with a sort of sea lion jump and wiggle movement.

"How's the water, Cheryl?"

"Good. How's the land?" Her voice sounded a bit like an operatic soprano on helium who felt the need to sing everything.

"Cold." Nico pulled Toni toward her. "Thanks so much for coming up. This is my friend, Toni."

"It's nice to meet you, Toni." She turned a bit and extended her hand to Toni.

Toni gently took Cheryl's hand, surprised how scaly and slippery it felt. She didn't quite know where to look. Unlike the children's movies, this mermaid wasn't actually wearing any sort of seashell covering. Not that she had anything resembling human breasts either. Toni tried not to stare, but it was unavoidable. She didn't even realize how long she had held on to Cheryl's hand until the mermaid gently pulled it away. "I'm sorry. It's… I have… I don't know what to do with this."

"It's fine, truly," Cheryl replied. "I understand. We get a lot of that."

"We?"

Cheryl smiled, and Toni got a look at the strange teeth in her mouth. They were more like the beakish tooth ridge of a dog-faced puffer, hard and sharp looking. However they didn't seem to hinder her speech. "This cove is home to many different creatures. We mermaids are only one portion. There aren't many of us left, but we found peace and safety here in Bear Ridge, so we stayed."

"How many of you are there?"

"About fifty. Soon to be fifty-three as some of us will be mothers soon. We would rather be a small community than a studied one.

We've seen what happens to the animals that humans think are interesting."

Toni continued to stare in wonder and then her eyes went wide, and she turned to Nico. "Wait. There are real mermaids. They really exist. Are there other things like that? Like unicorns or dragons or fairies?"

"In some form, most of those things at least have existed. Some still do. Maybe all of them. I can't promise you that what you think of when you say any of those things is what's real."

"What about mythological people?"

"Yes." Nico squeezed her hand gently. "All the things that you've been told, they're really real."

"Oh." She thought of Syn and Vor. Of Dr. Cait and Nana. Of saying goodbye to them all. "I've some apologies to make, don't I?"

"Tomorrow. You can save that for tomorrow." He pulled her close for a second before releasing her and stepping away. "Don't move."

Toni watched as he raced back toward the campfire and dug through his bag until he found what he was after. A fabric bag filled with something, Toni couldn't see what.

"I have gifts for you to take back to your village." He handed the bags to Cheryl. "Doc says it'll help when the babies come. He said your mother knows exactly what to do with it."

"Thanks. Someone will be back with a count when it happens, so Max can keep the books right."

"She sends her thanks for that." He took Toni's hand again. "Have a safe return home."

Cheryl nodded. "It was nice meeting you, Toni. I hope I count as magic enough for you."

"Oh, oh my goodness." She stammered through her discombobulated thoughts trying to find something appropriate. "You're amazing. I don't have a better word."

"I like amazing." The mermaid used her powerful arms and tail to make her way back into the water. "Merry Christmas."

"Merry Christmas," Nico and Toni called back as they watched her swim out into the ocean.

When they could no longer see the flash of her tail, Toni made her way back to the campfire and sat on the wooden bench. "I don't know what to do with this. How to come to terms with it. This isn't something I ever thought I'd come across."

"I know." Nico sat beside her and took her hand in his. "I understand how strange and difficult it must be."

"I don't think you do, really." She looked at him and her heart skipped a beat. He made her whole body want to dance and sing. He'd shown her a mermaid, a real one, and now, now he'd shown her real magic, the kind she had looked for all her life. He had shown her what her heart was for. He had more power than anyone she'd ever known had over her life.

"You're thinking too loud again. Why don't we put a stop to that before you run for the hills?" Nico leaned close, pressed his lips to hers and swept her back up into their own personal inferno.

Somehow, they made it back into the tent before their clothes dropped back on the canvas floor. Everywhere his fingers touched made fire burn beneath her skin. He made her feel things that both frightened and excited her. Her heart raced as his thumbs brushed her nipples so lightly the touch was like feathers and left her aching for more. Toni closed her eyes and let her hands wander over him, memorizing the shape of him, every plane and curve, for the long empty nights in her future. As they came together for what Toni knew had to be the last time, she couldn't help but cry. It was beautiful, it was perfect, it was everything she could ever want and everything she would never have. Nico was her forever and she was going to leave anyway. There were things she had to do that she couldn't do if she settled for perfection.

When he dropped her off at the inn, he tried to convince her to go home with him, to let him love her in a proper bed. Toni knew she couldn't do that. Once she went home with him, she knew she'd never leave his side.

Chapter Nine

Toni woke at dawn after far too little sleep. Nico definitely made sleep difficult. What they shared was beautiful, like a painting that should hang in the Louvre. There was no denying magic now, not after what they'd shared—even before she met Cheryl. It was a lot to come to terms with, living in a world where magic was really real. Where mermaids, pixies, and Valkyries really did exist. She had a lot to apologize for.

She knew she'd find at least one of her favorite women in the kitchen, so she got dressed and made her way down the stairs, pleased and more than a little surprised to find them both there. "Morning," she said with uncharacteristic shyness.

"Good morning." Syn smiled a little too brightly at her, as if wanting to foster their connection and still try to forget that Toni had basically scoffed at their entire life's history. "Did you have a good time yesterday?"

"I did. I also got to see some things." Toni sighed and wrapped her arms around Syn. "I'm so sorry I didn't believe you."

"Oh, honey, it's okay. I know how hard it can be to learn the truth of the world. We went through something sort of similar when we left Valhalla. Humans were not what we expected. You're all so much more than we could ever have known." Syn gave her another squeeze before letting her go. "Do you have any questions you want to ask?"

"No. Not really. I want to know all the things, but at the same time, you all tell me I'm going to forget everything anyway."

"Come, I want to show you something." Syn motioned for Toni to follow her but paused before they left the kitchen to pick up the internal phone, press a few numbers, and ask Vor to meet them in the basement. "We've been here a long time, so long that sometimes it's hard to remember that there's a bigger world out there. Sure, we see the news and movies and most of the time, we even get cable, but that's not the same as seeing the state of the world, is it?"

"Not really. There is a lot of awful out there, but there's a lot of wonderous beauty too." She followed Syn down the steps and into the large storage room. The armor she'd seen before was no longer in boxes but fitted to two dress forms, shined and dusted. "These are so cool. I mean, they were cool before I knew the truth of them. They're even cooler now."

Toni stepped toward them, really looking at them for the first time. The metal was etched with runes and marked by scars. "Were you in a lot of battles?"

"Oh yes. All of the battles of our people, in some way or another, for so long I couldn't even begin to quantify it." She sighed and looked a bit wistful.

"Why did you leave?"

Vor stepped into the storage room. "Because we wanted to be married. We could be together, but our friends, our leadership, did not want to see us make promises to each other in the way that man and woman have made promises to each other for centuries. We accepted that for too long a time. We did our duties, our jobs, content to be together even if we couldn't be married, and everyone was happy with that until they weren't."

"Rather than cause problems, we left." Syn smiled, but it was a tight, sad smile that didn't reach her eyes at all.

"I'm sorry you felt you had to do that. I imagine it was hard to leave the place you've called home for so many years."

"It was, but it was harder to stay there and not be able to be who we are." Vor rubbed at the armor, shining it. "It's been worth being away to be with the love of my life."

Syn blushed bright red, all the way to the tips of her ears. "Bear Ridge wasn't always home, but really, it's the *right* home. This place we've built, this life we've built, it is perfect for us. Sure, the people we meet leave and don't remember us per se, but I truly believe that they remember the things they've learned here. I believe they take some of the magic from this place into their hearts to share with others."

"That's a beautiful thought, and it's a shame that there's no way to know the truth of it."

"Not without them coming back to us. Some have though." Syn went deeper into the room to a box marked "1960s" and plucked out a photo album. "We went a bit camera crazy in the early days of photography and took pictures of everything and everyone for years. Sometimes we don't realize that someone has been here before until they remind us. We've had one couple that finds themselves here at least every three years or so. If they come back again, I imagine it'll be to stay next time."

"Why?"

"She has Alzheimer's and, when she's here, with Doc Cait and the powers of this place, it's much less pronounced. The downside to that is also that she remembers her friends and family and gets homesick. We love the Jenkins family and hopefully we'll see them again soon." She flipped through the album until she came to the picture she wanted. "This is them the first time they came to Bear Ridge."

The picture was of a middle-aged couple, arm in arm, with huge smiles on their faces, looking happy and serene.

Syn moved to another box and pulled out another album, flipping through it until she found the next picture of the Jenkins couple and then the next. "We've had a number of repeat visitors over the years and I guess I'm showing you these mostly because I have to hope that you'll be like them too and that we'll see you again someday."

Toni closed her eyes against the emotions she felt. "I hope that too."

"Oh, look here." Vor pulled out an album from another box. "This is when we remodeled. The awnings were getting so old that we didn't have a choice anymore."

Vor showed the picture and for a second, Toni saw the awning, but then a familiar face caught her eye and froze her heart. "Do you remember that couple?"

"Who? The ones walking past?" Vor looked a little closer. "I'm sorry, honey, I don't. I don't think they stayed at the inn though. Do you know them?"

"Those are my parents. Look, she's pregnant with me." Toni pointed to her mother's baby bump.

"So, in a way, you have been here before." Syn peeled the photo carefully from its sticky corners and looked closer at it. "Yeah, I don't think they stayed with us, but we can check the ledger easily enough. I think you should have this."

Toni took the photo and stared at it while Vor and Syn dug through the box and flipped through large, leather-bound ledgers for the time around when that picture was taken. "I'm sorry, honey, I don't see any Bells in here. If they stayed any length of time in Bear Ridge, it would have been at the hotel on the other side of town."

"Thank you. Thank you both so much. For everything." Tears welled up in her eyes. "I think I want to head over there and see if anyone remembers them."

"Good luck, Toni. I know how much it would mean to you to find them."

"Do you want to borrow the inn's car? It's too cold a day for that long of a walk." Syn took Toni's arm in hers. "I'll write the directions down for you."

"Are you sure?"

"Of course we are. Bear Ridge is a small town, but it's still quite the trek on foot even on nice days." They left the basement and Syn handed her a slip of paper with directions and a set of keys. "It's not a pretty thing but it is a four-wheel drive."

"It'll get me where I need to go." Toni kissed her cheek. "Thank you. Thank you both for understanding."

Toni climbed up into the ancient, black-panel van, feeling more than a bit like BA Baracus. The drive was pretty easy but much longer than she'd thought it would be. She was grateful not to have had to walk the distance. She passed the Greek restaurant Nico had taken her to, a book store, an antique store, and a few storefronts that weren't readily identifiable. She couldn't help but wonder how they got their supplies and inventory. Magic, Nico would tell her. Now, she had to believe him. Whatever power built the city and drew her citizens in kept them happy and supplied somehow. Toni couldn't help but wonder why.

The hotel was a five-story square building with the occasional balcony jutting out. Its gray stone face matched the other buildings on the block, looking both old and extraordinarily well kept. The doorman was dressed in a pressed and starched formal uniform complete with white gloves and crisp hat. Toni parked in an open lot across the street and made her way to him, photo in hand.

"What can I help you with this evening, miss?" he asked her, hands clasped in front of him.

"I'm not sure if you can, but you might be able to help me find someone who could." She held the picture up. "I'm hoping to find someone who can tell me if this couple stayed here. It would have been the early 1990s."

"Let me take a look. I've worked here since well before that." He looked at the photo and smiled sadly. "They're a lovely couple but I don't recall them. If you go to the front desk and ask for Georgia, she can check the records if you like."

"Thank you so much." She held the picture to her chest and went through the ornate wooden door the doorman held open for her.

At the front desk, a young girl stood trying to look busier than she probably was. She too wore a sharp uniform but hers was softer and less bundled as she wasn't expected to stand outside for her whole shift. "Can I help you?"

"The doorman suggested I ask for Georgia?"

"Give me a second." The woman picked up a phone and dialed a number and waited a moment before speaking. "Ms. Campbell, Henry sent a young woman to speak to you." She hung up the phone. "If you could have a seat over there, she'll be right with you. Can I get you a coffee or a tea while you're waiting?"

"Oh, don't go to any trouble on my account."

"It's no trouble at all."

"Coffee, please then. Thank you."

The girl smiled brightly and pointed in the direction of a pleasant seating area. The couches and chairs were smooth brown leather, softer than any calfskin Toni had ever come across. The colors were brilliantly neutral with a splash of deep burgundy in the throw pillows and tiny flowers in the great woven rug. It was a comfortable and beautiful space that smelled faintly of oranges.

The young girl brought her coffee on a shining silver tray in a delicate china cup with saucer. It was all rich, opulent, and upscale and exactly the opposite of any place she could see her wild-child wanderer parents staying. The coffee was good but still nowhere near as good as Nana's.

"Excuse me, miss?" A sweet, melodic voice had Toni turning slightly. The woman it belonged to was older than Toni expected.

The voice sounded nearly childlike, but the woman was definitely at least seventy. "I'm told you are looking for me?"

"Are you Georgia?"

"I am. How can I help you?" She sat down in a chair next to the couch.

"I was wondering if you could tell me if these people ever stayed here in your hotel. It would have been in late 1992 or early 1993?" She held the photograph out to the woman who peered at it.

"Hm. What was the name?"

"Bell. Dave and Joan Bell."

"Have a seat, relax, and give me a few minutes to check the books. They don't look familiar to me, but they might still be in the books. Enjoy your coffee and I'll see what I can find."

The woman walked away and left Toni by herself in the waiting area. She was a little jittery, trying to keep hold of the hope that they really had been here, but she knew that the Beacon Hotel was pretty much the opposite of their likely accommodations. If they'd stayed at all, they'd probably pitched a tent or stayed in the Harvester. She knew that—but still, she tried.

It was only ten minutes before Georgia emerged with the news that Toni had expected but also a hand-drawn map that would get her to the local campground and a man named Emmet who Georgia said remembered everything and everybody ever. Toni thanked her profusely and headed out to find one Emmet Lance with hope in her heart and her fingers crossed.

The campground was a bit more out of the way. Without Georgia's map, she probably would have gotten lost near Bear Lake. The campground itself was unmarked except by the cute log-cabin style general store where Georgia said she would find Emmet. Toni parked the inn's van and made her way up the steps. She didn't reach the door before it opened for her. The old man was old and weathered and looked quite angry. "Mr. Lance?"

"You must be the girl Georgia sent out." His voice was softer and kinder than his face would elude.

"Toni. Toni Bell." She held out her hand before she realized that he didn't have a right hand. Instead, he offered his left. "Sorry."

He laughed lightly. "It happens all the time. Come on in, let's see if we can't figure this out. Georgia said you were looking for records from '90, or thereabouts."

"Right." Toni followed him into the store, warmed by an ancient potbellied stove that was flanked by two hand-carved wooden chairs. She sat in the one he left available for her. "I appreciate any help you can give me."

"I take it you've lost your parents then?"

"Several years ago, now, yes."

"I'm sorry to hear that. I know losing people we love can be incredibly difficult. Especially when you're so young."

"Thank you." She held out the photograph to him. "I know Syn and Vor didn't actually meet them and, I'll be honest with you, the Beacon isn't really the kind of place my parents would stay. They would have been driving an old International Harvester. Well, I guess it wasn't nearly as old then."

"Oh. You're the girl that had the accident in front of the diner. I heard about that. I'd imagine Kevin should nearly have the repairs finished."

She nodded. "It's supposed to be done today."

"He does good work." The man took the photo and stared at it for a moment. "I'm sorry, Ms. Bell. I remember everyone who's stayed here since I was ten, and these people didn't stay here. Maybe they drove straight through. Most people do, really. They might get turned around for a second or were looking for some gas or lunch and went on their way after they found it. That's likely what happened here. I wish I had better news for you."

"Me too. But thank you so much for trying." She took the photo back and tucked it in her pocket. She had one more possibility. She'd wanted to find a different way, but she'd crossed off each other option. "Have a Merry Christmas, Mr. Lance."

"A Merry Christmas to you too, Miss Bell." He walked her back out to the van and stood watch as she retraced her steps, following the directions back the way she'd come. All the way to the inn. She left the keys on the front desk and headed back out on foot.

With picture in hand, Toni knocked on the locked door of Max's shop. It was closed, but Toni did not care. The raven above the door grumbled and fluffed himself but did not fly away or try to chase her off. She was moderately grateful for that.

Max opened the door and confusion passed over her face. "I wasn't expecting you tonight."

"Amazing. The all-seeing can't see everything."

"I am not all-seeing anything, and I never claimed to be." Ice slid through her voice and the temperature dropped another five degrees toward the wrong side of zero.

"You should have told me. You should have said something." She waved the picture in front of Max's face. "They were here. Years ago, they were here, and you said nothing."

"What? Who was here."

"My parents. This picture was in storage at the Bear Ridge Inn. They were here, and no one told me."

Max snatched the picture so she could get a better look at the couple. "These people may have been in Bear Ridge for a while many years ago, but I honestly don't remember them."

"How could you not remember them? If you talked to them, you'd remember them. I know it. If they had walked past your shop, they would have come in if only to see how you had it set up on the inside."

The anger in Max's eyes disappeared. "Honey, there are a lot of people who come through this town and stay for a while—or not— and live and laugh and love here… or not. I have been here for so long I can barely remember anywhere else. I don't think you understand how old I really am."

"You can't be that old, Max. You might be pushing fifty, if you have the best skin regimen on the planet."

Max laughed brightly. "That might be the kindest thing I've ever been told. Do you remember the conversation we had a few days ago, about magic gathering here and magic people gathering here?"

"Yes."

"I'm one of those people."

"No. No, no, no. Not you too. First my ladies, then Nana, and now *you*? The only thing gathering here is delusion. You're all fucking crazy. And I'm crazy for listening to this shit." Max didn't so much as drop her strange smile. "Okay then, who? Who exactly are you?"

"I've had many names in my time and sometimes they like to split me up into other names, depending on your corner of mythology. My favorite name has been Macha."

"Shortened to Max."

"I've lived longer than humans have been civilized. I've existed for as long as anything in existence can remember. None of us remembers a time before us."

"So, you're what? A goddess? Like Syn and Vor?"

"That's what they say, more or less. I was a bit more popular in my heyday, but yes."

Toni made a strange sort of grunting sound. "You really don't remember them?"

"I'm sorry, but no. If I remembered all the people I've met, you wouldn't live long enough for me to name them all. Honestly, when you leave, I won't remember you after a while either, no matter how interesting or charming or whatever other words you like to think you are." The coldness came back a little, sharpening the disappointment. "I can't give you what you want. I can't bring them back. I can't contact them. I can't teach you how. They are dead and long gone and it's time for you to actually live the life you've been given instead of spending it trying to find them. They are gone. And I think you should go now."

Max stepped out of the main showroom and Toni heard her go into her kitchen suite. She also heard the definitive snick of the door closing. She held the photo close and left the store under the watchful eye of the large bird who squawked at her, almost scolding her.

"I don't need it from you as well. None of you understand. Maybe *I* don't even understand." Toni looked up at the big bird. "Goodbye, Mr. Raven. I know I'll never know another bird quite like you. You're incredible and I'm sorry that I'll forget you too."

The large bird dropped down from his perch above the door to sit on the snow-dusted copper dragon's shoulder, nearly at eye level with Toni. He tutted and whirred at her, fluffing his feathers, shaking his tail.

Toni moved close to him, petting him softly and leaning her face in close to his. "I really am going to miss you, silly bird."

"Silly bird?"

"I swear you understand every word I say to you. But I guess you must also be a little bit of magic." She sighed heavily. "I have to go. I have places to be... to see. I have people to meet and oceans to swim in. I'm not built to stay in one place."

Mr. Raven looked at her, staring intently.

"I'm sorry. I can't be that person. No for you, not even for him." Toni wiped her eyes and started down the sidewalk at a run. Kevin promised her truck would be ready and she could only cross her fingers and hope that was the case.

She had finished crying by the time she reached the garage and she couldn't help but smile as her father's pride and joy pulled into the lot, she assumed after a test run. It sounded perfect. She hoped it ran that way too.

"Did she pass the test?"

Kevin climbed down out of the driver's seat and tossed her the key. "Why don't you tell me? Give her a spin and double check and then we'll settle up."

Getting behind the wheel felt a lot like finally coming home. The Harvester was really the only home she'd ever really known, after all. Toni drove it around the little town, purposefully not looking at any of the people she passed, even though she'd come to know most of them. She did her best to ignore the sadness and the melancholy that threatened to settle into her heart at the thought of saying goodbye to more than a few of them. She pulled her dad's dog tags and her mother's octopus pendant out of her pocket and hung them from the rearview mirror, now finally back where they belonged

When she got back to Kevin's garage, she handed over the cash. It was a hit to her nest egg, but there was no way she was going to ask Nico to pay for any bit of it. She did not want that to be the last memory he had of her. She could pack up and sneak out and never tell anyone. It would be easier. She could disappear and let them all forget about her. Maybe the town worked that way too, helping those who stayed forget those who left. Maybe Nico would forget her when she forgot him.

Instead of driving to the inn to get her things, she drove to Nico's house. There were no lights in the windows, no sign of him or his dog. Wherever they were, it wasn't there. Maybe it was better to not say goodbye. Maybe it would be easier to leave.

Toni riffled through her things until she found a piece of paper and a pen and wrote him a note.

Nico,

I'm sorry to say goodbye like this, but we both knew this day would come. Thank you for showing me what magic is, for making me believe again.

Toni

She thought about using *that* word—the L word—but she knew it would only make things worse. She tucked the note in his front door and headed back to the inn to pack up her things. It wouldn't take long; she'd learned as a little girl that traveling light was best. It was impossible to lose that which you did not have. At least, that's what her mom told her when she was small and lost her favorite stuffed cat somewhere near Myrtle Beach.

Chapter Ten

Toni ignored Syn and Vor's protests as she put her things back where they belonged, tucked into their proper cubbies, snapped into their proper holders. It was going to be good to get back to normal. It was what she'd always said she would do. She had beaches to comb, waves to ride, songs to write. Christmas didn't mean anything to her anymore. She wasn't built to settle down. She was made for bigger things.

"If you won't stay for Christmas, will you at least take your present with you?" Syn pressed a small, brightly wrapped package into Toni's trembling hands. "Please."

"You've already done too much."

"This is for us as much as you. When you leave, you won't remember us, but maybe you'll remember something of us fondly." She pressed her lips to Toni's cheek. "We are so glad you came, even if you aren't staying. Our lives are better for having met you. You're going to do wonderful things out in the world, even if you don't see it."

"You two are too much." Toni pulled the paper free and bit back a laugh at the antique beaded spider in the pretty box. "A tinsel spider for me? I love it."

"It'll hang from your mirror as well as it would any tree." Vor pulled Toni into a bear hug. "We will miss you terribly."

"Thank you." Toni gently pushed away and climbed up into the truck. She didn't trust herself to speak but waved at them as she drove off in the direction she'd come into Bear Ridge. If Nico was right, the best way out was the way she'd come in.

She almost made it to the rock that marked the entrance to Bear Ridge. She almost escaped without saying a word to him—but no, he really did know her. Nico stood in the middle of the road with Juni on a proper leash beside him. She pulled to a stop about four feet away.

"I'm not getting out of the truck," Toni yelled through her open window.

"You're a coward, Toni Bell."

"And you're absolutely right. I can't take losing someone else. I can't do it."

"If that were really true, you'd stay. Once you leave here, you'll forget us all—me, Syn and Vor, Max."

"Max will be damned glad I'm gone."

"Believe it or not, she really likes you. Toni, I don't want you to go." He stepped closer, not stepping out of the road but clearly wanting to be closer. "Please stay. I don't want any forever but you. I love you."

"That's why I have to go." That much she said out loud. She knew telling him the truth would only make her absence hurt more.

"I can't even tell you how much you'll regret leaving, because you won't even admit it to yourself." There were tears in his eyes, in his voice. "Can I kiss you goodbye?"

"No." Toni shook her head and started creeping forward slowly. If he kissed her again, she'd never let him go, and she *had* to let him go. "Move, Nico. Let me go."

"Wait until tomorrow and I'll come with you. Even if you won't wait, I'll come with you. I don't care as long as we're together."

"I can't do that to you. You belong here." She felt the tears welling up in her eyes but she refused to let them fall.

"I belong with you. I really do love you, Toni." She heard the resignation in his voice as he accepted her decision. "You won't remember me, or what we have, but maybe you'll remember that someone, somewhere, loves you. Maybe you'll even remember someday that you loved me too." Nico stepped off the road with Juni and let her pass. When she started driving again, he watched her leave and made no move to stop her.

Toni drove headlong into the rolling cloud bank, tears streaming down her face. He wasn't wrong. She was a coward. Motivated only by fear and longing and grief and something she could never put words to. Toni stopped the car, watching the fog around her turn to snow; the same snow that had brought her in had come to usher her back out again. She closed her eyes and laid her head on the steering wheel.

The sound of bells approaching startled her. The booming laugh sent a chill through her entire body. Toni rolled down her window to hear it better and could not contain the joy that bloomed in her heart. If she'd learned anything in Bear Ridge it was that nothing was impossible or unbelievable.

"Little Toni Bell. I haven't seen you in years. Not since you stopped believing, anyway."

"Wait, you're not..."

Santa himself approached her car, leading his team of reindeer through the snow behind him. He looked older, happier, and wiser than she expected. He laughed again, and his eyes twinkled. "You thought I was my son, that he was me. No, but he's getting better at impersonating me every year."

"So, you don't forget Bear Ridge?"

"How can I? There are many little children here who believe more purely in magic and miracles. Adults too."

"Magical people would tend to believe in other magical people." She nodded. "This is a damned strange world."

"You're not wrong. Like attracts like, the world tends to work that way. Well, except when it doesn't." He nodded, his silky white beard bobbing against his chest. "What have you decided?"

"What?"

"You're torn between two wishes and you can only have one," he said.

"What would you do? If you were me?"

"It doesn't matter what I would do. This is a choice only you can make, and you know it."

Toni closed her eyes again and thought of Nico, except she couldn't picture his face or remember his dog's name or the touch of his lips on her skin or the taste of sea salt on his. She knew only love. She was losing him, and she didn't want to. She *never* wanted to.

With a wish and a snap of gloved fingers, the Harvester was turned the right way around. The closer she got, the more clearly, she could see what she almost lost. The silhouette of him and Juni— oh she remembered Juni—still standing beside the welcome rock filled her heart to the brim. She'd never wanted a home, never believed she could hold on to it, that it would stay, but this time, maybe the risk was worth it.

"You get lost?" Nico practically vibrated standing next to her car.

"Almost, Nico. Almost." Toni parked the truck, flung open the door and launched herself into his arms. "I figured out what I want for Christmas."

Nico put his hands on either side of her face and stared into her eyes as Juni yipped and pranced beside them. "You did?"

Toni nodded. "You." She kissed him and her whole life fell into place. "I don't want to lose you or forget you, or Vor, or Syn, or Mr. Raven."

"Mr. Raven?"

"I think he's Max's. He's always hanging out on her sign and he comes to visit me sometimes."

Nico started laughing. "Mr. Raven. He's definitely not Max's or anyone's pet for that matter. You call Death's favorite immortal psychopomp Mr. Raven? Well, I don't know about him, but I know Vor and Syn will be thrilled you're staying."

"They didn't want me to go in the first place." She pulled him close, leaning her ear on his chest to hear his heart beat and feel it match hers. "Death's what now?"

"Psychopomp. He delivers the souls of the dead, traveling with them to their destination."

"But I'm not dead, right? The mayor said I wasn't."

Nico laughed. "No, you are definitely not dead. I promise. Maybe he knows how much you've lost and wanted to be some comfort."

"That's a much nicer explanation." She nodded.

"I need to know something. Why did you want to leave so badly?" He pulled her back far enough to look into her eyes. "The truth, Toni."

"I've spent my entire adult life on the move, trying to see all the things my parents wanted to see, do all the things they wanted to do. Max is right. I've never lived my own life. I've been living theirs. I've been trying so hard to find them that I lost me. Here, I know who I am. With you, I know exactly who I am, and I don't want to give that up to spend a few more empty years bouncing from town to town looking for something I'm never going to find anyway because it's all right here."

She wrapped her arms around him and pulled him in close again. "I love you, Nicodemous. I really do."

He whooped as he lifted her up and spun her around. He was smart enough to drop the leash but not quite smart enough to avoid the jumping and leaping puppy paws as Juni joined in their joy with yips and barks of her own, sending Toni and Nico into a fit of giggles as they fell into the snow only to get smothered by a wiggly, licky pibble who wasn't quite sure which of them to love.

"Feel like going to my mother's house for Christmas lunch?"

"I guess meeting the parents is inevitable at this point, isn't it?"

"There's something you should probably know about my mother." Nico helped Toni stand up and they brushed the snow from each other. "You remember how I said she tends to be obsessed with literature?"

"Vaguely, sure." She stopped moving to look at him.

"Yeah, well, I know Max told you who she is, and Doc Cait, and Syn and Vor."

"Is your mom a goddess too?" Toni's acceptance of Bear Ridge was complete. The truth of the place and its people bloomed in her heart and nothing could surprise her now.

"Worse. She's a muse."

"Huh. Okay. If she's a muse, like a mythological muse, she can certainly appreciate a good story, and I have lots of them. None quite as good as ours so far, but I think she'll like me even if I'm not Wohpe." She accepted it as truth and let her doubt go.

"I know she will." He scooped up Juni and got into the passenger seat of the truck.

Toni started driving, feeling like she wasn't chasing anything. She smiled and wondered what color her mist cloud would be now if she looked into Max's magic mirror.

ALSO BY SARAH WAGNER

Hunter's Crossing
Eldercynne Rising

ABOUT THE AUTHOR

Born in Denver, Colorado, Sarah Wagner got her first taste of people watching from inside the seventy-five gallon tank that served as her playpen in her parents' tropical fish store. She liked it so much, she continued to people watch whenever she could and it has led to some very interesting characters.

She got her first taste of science fiction early, thanks to her devoted Trekkie of a mom. Science fiction was her gateway genre, leading to fantasy, horror, and superheroes. She hopes to be able to pass this deep love along to her children.

Sarah spends her time torn between the worlds in her head and this one. Her husband and two sons do a wonderful job keeping her relatively grounded in this one. She writes in a little corner where clutter breeds and dust bunnies find refuge.

In what free time she can eke out, she loves to read and drink coffee. She also runs an autism support group. You can find Sarah's short stories in a wide variety of publications including the Sha'Daa anthologies, Ruins Metropolis, and her collection, Hardwired Humanity.

You can find Sarah online at
www.sarahewagner.com,
queenofmygeekdom.wordpress.com
Twitter @Shade53
Instagram @shadeinink

Did you enjoy this book? Drop us a line and say so. We love to hear from readers, and so do our authors. To connect, visit www.boroughspublishinggroup.com online, send comments directly to info@boroughspublishinggroup.com. Friend us on Facebook and follow us on Twitter and Instagram. And be sure to sign up for our newsletter for surprises and new releases in your favorite subgenres of romance.

Are you an aspiring writer? Check out www.boroughspublishinggroup.com/submit and see if we can help you make your dreams come true.